Brendan Connell was born in Santa Fe, New Mexico, in 1970. His works of fiction include *Unpleasant Tales* (Eibonvale Press, 2013), *The Architect* (PS Publishing, 2012), *Lives of Notorious Cooks* (Chômu Press, 2012), *Miss Homicide Plays the Flute* (Eibonvale Press, 2013), *Cannibals of West Papua* (Zagava, 2015), and *Clark* (Snuggly Books, 2016).

Pleasant Tales

Brendan Connell

With an Introduction by Justin Isis

Contents

Inauguration of the Pleasantness

What is the opposite of Horror?

It cannot be, as is often thought, an unreflective grounding in the everyday, the kind of consensus-seeking Social Realism favored by whoever currently maintains the Canon™. Inasmuch as Horror is a scalar value, a jerking left into the negative zone of the Uncanny, then its opposite cannot be the zero point neutrality of the merely Real; it requires, instead, a state just as heightened, equal but opposite. This state, it seems clear, has until now been evoked much less in literature than its superficially menacing but commercially profitable reflection, but for some time it has been gaining momentum in certain subterranean channels of its own, unobserved and mostly unsuspected until the publication of the present volume. This state is *the Pleasant*.

It's been noted that a worldview often achieves its greatest prominence just as it is about to decline. This seems an appropriate description of what could variously be termed the cosmic horror or Lovecraftian mode, which some would claim to be undergoing a renaissance, but which seems more strictly appropriate to the years of its origin than to the early decades of the 21st century. At the time when this mode was still fresh, the scientific revelations of Darwin and Einstein, the mass devastations of the World Wars, and the changing social attitudes brought about by rapidly advancing technology all hastened the decline of the already enfeebled anthropocentric view of literature. The novelty of the approach was to suggest that increased scientific understanding would lead, not to greater sanity and social harmony as H.G. Wells would have had us believe, but to an unceremonious expulsion into a universe that was at best infinitely and inhospitably vast, and at worst populated with forces wholly destructive to human life and meaning. And as the 20th century progressed, the various voices of Anxiety, Absurdity and Exhaustion joined the chorus. The critical quarter took part too, with academic writings focused on the radical contingency of human values. By the turn of the 21st century, this mode had become something of a default, degrading into a reflexive apocalypticism suitable for the comic books, video games and blockbuster films that had arisen to recuperate its insights and render them safe for the capitalist production line. In other words, this mode has become shorthand for "seriousness," and has now reached its Mannerist nadir.

It's possible to imagine the Pleasant incubating all the while, beneath a toadstool perhaps, like some shadowy fairy embryo. The fairy or bright blinking goblin of the Pleasant, youthful and shy, has until now only peeked through the pages of a scattered band of authors who would at first seem to have little in common: Colette, John Cowper Powys, Jippensha Ikku, Robert Walser, Mario Vargas Llosa, Italo Svevo. But there is nothing here like a school, and the glimpses of the Pleasant in their works are just that: brief sightings, usually unverified and likely to have been taken for something else entirely. The Pleasant is distinct from the whimsical, the absurd, the comical and the farcical. The Pleasant is not pastoral; neither is it realism in the sense that the term is usually meant; neither is it fantasy. A few of the works of Quentin S. Crisp come perilously close to embodying the Pleasant in full flower (the story "Italianetto," and parts of the novel *Blue on Blue*). But nowhere has concentrated Pleasantness been felt until now.

In 2010 Brendan Connell published *Unpleasant Tales*. Unlike many of his more workshopped peers, Connell had, in the service of style, sensibly discarded plot, character, "arcs," "craftsmanship," and most of the other appurtenances of modern commercial fiction. In their place was an emphasis on the historical extrusions of decadence, or what might be termed a Neo-Decadent expression of classical decadent themes. *Unpleasant Tales* thus succeeded in its objectives, but in a sense it succeeded too well. Eight-year-old boys and girls reading it were stricken with a profound sense of disquietude that occasionally interfered with their delectation of the conveniences of the modern Industrial Age. To be unpleasant is at heart to be uncivilized, and nothing uncivilized can long retain the attention of an English-language readership. After realizing the crudeness of the Unpleasant and its even more boorish and self-aggrandizing cousin, the Weird (now a reformed New™ genre of sorts, with its own tedious orthodoxies and compound eyes fixed on the Hollywood Prize), Connell went through a prolonged spiritual crisis. He drank mostly black barley tea, fed himself on figs and prickly pears, and observed the desert, the sky. Through rigorous training he achieved an enviable abdominal definition. He wandered the streets at night playing Tetris on a vintage Game Boy. In the end he arrived at the Pleasant through mostly non-rational and extra-literary means.

The Pleasant as manifested through Connell's stories is unconcerned with any teenage hysterics, with any of the plunging, swooning theatrics of Modernist ecstasy. Character and self as generally understood are not important; neither is plot in the standard sense. The Pleasant mode is at once atmospheric yet deeply detached, expansive yet leanly impersonal. Blissfully unmarked by the cross-hatchings of programmatic psychological realism, it is in a sense a transpersonal literature, albeit one more spiritually complete than its predecessors. It is manifestly not a critique, in that it does not perceive anything in existence to be lacking. Its characters are human in the same sense that figures in premodern literature are human, while still striking us as recognizable inhabitants of the present.

The instinctive philosophical position of the Pleasant can be defined as a kind of super-correlationism. The universe is not inimical to human life, nor even indifferent to it; rather, the universe dotes on us like a grandfather, wheezing and rocking in infinitely relaxed decrepitude, patient and amused, blinking its endless eyes or stars. A benevolent animism quickens its rhythms. The characters are not situated in their settings like actors on a stage; rather the settings emerge directly from the characters, or can be considered as the expressions of everything they are not consciously aware of knowing, but are always remembering in some vague, distracted way. There is something grotesquely excessive about the Pleasant, yet perfectly natural—and in this it is the perfect counterpart to Horror, because it evokes exactly as much of an inhumanly positive seizure of Meaning as its opposite does a negative or malevolent seizure through estrangement.

Connell seems to be telling us: the Human in the 21st century has become estranged from estrangement. The period of Anxiety, Absurdity and Exhaustion was akin to the momentary disillusionment felt by a child discovering the literal non-existence of Santa Claus. For a brief moment the child became a cynical atheist concerned with "truth" and perturbed by vast doubts; eventually, though, the realization set in that the child's parents were in fact doing the hard work of depositing the vintage Game Boys and brightly-colored toothbrushes under the ornament-laden tree. And just as the Claus scenario functions structurally as a form of home invasion, so the child or reader will come to anticipate that tingling moment when the Pleasant comes crawling down the chimney of the everyday, dressed in its ancestral costume, depositing fresh novelties wrapped in cheap tinsel. *Pleasant Tales* is a vision of the Human utterly at home in the universe, sinking into mildness as into an old armchair. The Pleasant is coming, and it fully intends to crawl headfirst into your safe space. Be sure to keep your metaphysics clean, and leave out a plate of cookies.

—Justin Isis

Pleasant Tales

Green You and Green Me and Green Apples and Black Crows

1.

"I wish I could get into modern rock music. Hip hop and reggae and shit hits me in the feels, but modern rock . . ."

"EPIC FAIL!!!"

"Yeah."

"The death of grunge."

"What?"

"Nothing. Was just remembering how back in high school my dealer would toss a tennis ball with a slit in it out of his bedroom window. I'd stick money in it and toss it back up and he would throw it back down with whatever I paid for."

"Holy fuck, I knew a guy who did this with potato chip bags."

Raymond Feroze took another hit of the joint and squinted his eyes.

"Good weed," he said, thinking *what element could be blocking during the peak trying to channel my inner, yeah, um, animal feel/think/smell like if I were a dog nose always wet myrcene on the blood-brain on the mind of a dwarf high anything more than pets can help amazed what I can smell conserve my animal existence I can smell the dirt, standing up, and smell the critters in the woods and mangos and the girl in the apartment below whose boyfriend plays the kick drum.*

"You ripped?" Billy Glandzk asked.

"Ripped enough. You?"

"I'm more hungry than ripped."

Raymond nodded his head, got up and went to the kitchen. A minute later he came back with two Mutsu apples.

"This is all I got, but they're organic."

Billy didn't mean to be impolite, but he couldn't help making a face.

Raymond set one of the apples down on the coffee table in front of him and then started eating the other. Billy could smell it from where he sat and the smell, a pentyl pentanoate nightmare, nauseated him. He hated apples with a passion. In fact, the only thing he hated more than apples was bananas.

"You don't want yours?" Raymond asked.

"No, I hate apples."

"That's not cool."

"Yeah?"

"Hate's not good."

"Yeah."

"You know what they say?"

"Who?"

"Science."

"Huh?"

"The less weed you smoke, the less likely you are to eat an apple."

"WTF?"

"All weed gives you the munchies, right?"

"All the weed I've smoked does."

"So, everything that isn't weed, doesn't give you the munchies."

"You mean if I smoke something that isn't weed it won't give me the munchies?"

"I'm talking deeper science. You smoke a doobie and don't want an apple; but I think smoking it did give you the munchies cuz you said so."

"Yeah, weed gives me the munchies. That's it."

"Well, since some people who have the munchies eat green apples, it's only logical that if you smoke weed it increases the probability that you'll eat a green apple. It's like, even if we have never observed the size of a joint, we can, according to inductive process, conclude that all joints when smoked will cause the munchies and will make you go get the honey BBQ chicken strip sandwich and maybe even replace the BBQ sauce with the jalapeño sauce from the Monterey melt or ask for the grilled fajita veggies and maybe replace the fries with onion rings, get a chocolate malt, and then go home and sleep, but eventually there won't be any BBQ chicken strip sandwich and you'll be eating a green apple."

"Yeah?"

"It's logic."

Billy scratched his right ear. Maybe Raymond had something. He did, after all, attend Columbia University as a Philosophy Major. He was pretty smart.

2.

That night, when Billy got back to his apartment in Newark, he made love to Plock Plock, his trim blonde sex doll, but did it without his usual enthusiasm.

He took a bong hit, popped two valerian capsules in his mouth, washing them down with carrot juice spiked with a dash of Monte Alban mezcal, and went to bed.

He kept dreaming that he was being molested by apples—pink, blue and red, but mostly green little sugar apple scenes fingering him before the juicy splashed with green apple shop regarding the smothered in babies apple juice foam apples particularly buttoned Nonpareil apples rolling over his feet attacking and smell coarse flesh lick her apple tips onanism very firm making him eat the core coitus baking with cinnamon by means of intense thought of buttoned Nonpareil apples or the brisk tasting apples rolling over him heavy hanging fruits smashing at his temples.

When he woke up the next morning, he made himself a cup of coffee, put on a Barrington Levy CD and rolled a joint. He had been doing the wake and bake ritual every day since he had been fifteen and it was for him something verging on the sacred.

Kush tampons are repeatedly pledged
Until he lays flat on the ground
Get up and smoke that big ass joint once more
And live free from having a brain
So shall bigbruthaman be faded as fuckkkk

He sat poised with the joint in one hand and a cobalt blue BiC lighter in the other, but he couldn't get apples out of his head.

"Raymond is about the most intelligent dude I know," he thought. "I mean, he might be right about the apple thing."

He felt panicked. He noticed that his left hand was shaking and that his right foot was tapping the ground like he was listening to electro house instead of mellow reggae.

He put the joint down, unlit, and then went and took the hottest shower he had ever had in his life.

After toweling himself off and blow-drying his long hair, he put on a pair of jeans and a when-life-gives-you-lemons-add-vodka T-shirt.

It was Saturday and he didn't have to work. Normally he spent his days off playing Minecraft and reading small press horror books. For some reason though, he didn't now feel like it. He looked around his apartment. It seemed dark. He suddenly realized there was only one window, and the venetian blinds covering it were closed. He opened them and saw two panes of dirty glass. He felt like crying.

"This place stinks," he said to himself.

3.

Billy cruised through the Holland Tunnel in his red Suzuki Jimny and into Manhattan.

He had decided to hang out in the city for a while, catch a matinee in the afternoon, try to get out of the blank ages, break fate, tell the funk to fuck off. As he drove along Canal Street, he felt invaded by a vague feeling of emptiness. He looked at the pedestrians and noticed that most of the men had short hair. Those that didn't seemed unclean and most of them looked like they were probably poor, or even homeless.

He took a left on Green Street and, after going a few blocks, saw a sign that said 'White Nectar Hair Salon'.

"Fuck it," he said, and pulled over.

The truth was that it had been a long time since he had had a haircut, and even longer since he had been to an actual barber or hair stylist. For the last few years he had just been letting one of his friends' sisters, a middle-aged Norwegian woman by the name of Unn, trim the ends in exchange for joints.

He opened the door and stepped inside.

Music was thumping away. There were three barber chairs. A small blonde woman stood behind one of them and was cutting the hair of a nineteen-year-old Public Policy major. The next chair (the middle) was occupied by a two-hundred-and-ten-pound male. Behind him a supple-bodied Type A personality was snipping away briskly with a pair of Yasaka opposing grip shears. The third and last chair was unoccupied and near it stood a free-spirit-confident-guy wearing a pair of DSQUARED[2] workwear jeans and a Boxfresh Stika Lumby cocktail print T-shirt. He was busy sending a text message on his iPhone, but looked up as a lion might from a downed and bloody antelope when Billy walked in.

Free Spirit motioned Billy towards the chair. Billy was about to ask how much a haircut was, but the obstreperous look the man cast on him made him decide not to. He sat down in the chair and told the man to cut it short.

The hairdresser kept pushing his crotch up against Billy's leg as the scissors sang their song:

> Away with shaggy back
> Let me pamper you LOL
> You can be brought like my guinea pigs
> There can be many haircut things
> Even a political statement
> Nothing but good cut too sexy!
> Sociology hair GreatClips suck hard
> What is more important is that you feel good?

When, forty-five minutes later, a mirror was put in front of his face, he hardly recognized himself. He looked almost as good as a Sinthetics William doll.

The hundred and ten dollars the stylist charged seemed like an awful lot, but Billy didn't want to seem cheap so he threw in a twenty dollar tip.

Without the long hair, his brain felt cool and alert. Thoughts moved through his head with lightning speed. He had had a pair of Maui Jim 103 Stingray sunglasses, but had broken them opening the refrigerator door a few months before. Now his cheap 'inspired by Prada' sunglasses suddenly seemed out of place on his face, so he went into a shop and bought a pair of Mykita Pierce 142s with champagne-colored frames for $357.72.

It felt good to be alive. Really good! As he walked to his Suzuki Jimny he smiled and said 'hello' to two different people he passed and one of them said 'hi' back.

After he got in his car, he pulled out his iPhone and, toggling to the Showtimes app, checked out what films were playing. There was a film starring Jake Gyllenhaal that he thought might be decent. He had liked Gyllenhaal in *Nightcrawler*, so decided to give it a try. It was playing at AMC Loews on 84th Street at 1:35 and it was still only 12:14, so he had plenty of time.

He turned the key in the ignition and the engine began to purr. He headed up Greene Street to Broome, took a left, veered onto Watts, took a left on Varick, took a right onto Canal, took a right on West Street, continued on to 11th Avenue, went towards 10th Avenue, took a right on West 14th Street, merged onto 10th Avenue, continued onto Amsterdam Avenue, turned left onto West 75th Street, and then took a right onto Broadway. He drove past the theater and started looking for a parking spot, but didn't find one until 87th Street.

He looked at his iPhone. It was 12:38.

He still had almost an hour to kill before the movie, so decided to get something to eat.

There was a Tal Bagels nearby, so he went in there and ordered chopped herring on a pumpernickel bagel and a bottle of Poland Spring water.

He sat down, unscrewed the top off the water bottle, took a drink, then took a bite of his bagel.

As he was eating, he noticed a young woman at another table in the corner, eating a salt bagel with Jarlsberg cheese while talking on her iPhone. A laptop bag was leaning against her chair.

While she was talking, an Irishman in his mid-thirties sat down at the table next to hers. He wasn't eating anything and Billy hadn't seen him order from the counter. The man pulled out a cheap-looking mobile phone and started looking at it, but Billy noticed that while he looked at his phone, his foot edged the young woman's laptop bag closer to him, so that soon the bag was actually behind her chair, where she couldn't see it. At that point, the Irishman leaned over, opened the bag and extracted a Toshiba Tecra Z50-BT1501.

Billy had seen how things were going, and before the Irishman had a chance to rise from his seat, rushed over and grabbed him around the neck with one arm.

"Drop it, fucker!" he cried out.

The man let go of the laptop and Billy let go of him and was then thrown to the floor as the man escaped.

A few people looked over with bland interest.

"OMG!" the young woman said. "Are you all right?"

Billy said that he was and got up off the floor.

"Thank you SO much!" the young woman said. "YOU SAVED MY LAPTOP!"

The young woman introduced herself as Kimberley Courtney and told him that the laptop had cost her $1,414 not fancy but beautiful so proud!!! So appreciation gratitude!!! She was tearing up, feeling *omigosh wiggly most important lesson maturity pitterpatterpitterpatter the courage better Brownian motion than cold plastic manipulating the vols.*

She had blonde hair and brown eyes and wore eyeliner and was sort of slim in the seat.

"I need to buy you a drink!" she said.

Billy would have rather seen the Jake Gyllenhaal movie, but didn't want to be impolite, so he accepted her invitation. He could always go to the next showing anyhow, and maybe after a drink the film would be more enjoyable. He hadn't seen a film without being baked in some time and was a little worried that without proper stimulation, the experience would be lackluster.

They went to a nearby bar and ordered gin and tonics.

She started talking about Gmail, Mary Poppins and child brides. She said she was studying to be a financial quantitative analyst at NYU but was also interested in fabric and material patternmaking.

"I really believe in tenacity," she said. "It's okay to sometimes say that you're sorry. But it's important that we're all nice to ourselves. That's why I always take myself out to lunch. I sometimes wish I was French so that I could kiss people on the cheeks. If you feel love, you should share it, don't you think?"

Billy nodded his head. It occurred to him that he had been letting her carry the weight of the conversation, so he started talking vaguely about Thomas Ligotti and Alexander Rosenberg and then, realizing that he was losing her, told her a story about how when he was a little boy he had fallen in love with his teddy bear whose name was Sam.

"That's so cool!" she said enthusiastically. "It's so rare to meet a guy who's willing to show his emotions!"

Billy gave a vague smile and signaled for the bartender to bring them another round.

By the end of the second drink, he realized he was hungry. He had only eaten half his bagel.

"I think I understand where you're coming from," Kimberley said. "I only had a few bites of my salt bagel with Jarlsberg cheese before that CREEP grabbed my laptop."

Before he knew it, they were at Panna II on 1st Avenue. It was a BYOB restaurant, so Billy went to the liquor store downstairs and bought a bottle of California Pinot Noir, which he thought would probably go good with Indian food.

Kimberly smiled when Billy poured wine into her glass.

"I don't usually drink during the day," she said, "but somehow I feel——"

"Yeah, I know what you mean," Billy replied.

The restaurant had been Kimberly's suggestion and it turned out that her apartment was just a few blocks away, on East 10th Street, so after eating she invited him up, fixed a pot of rosehip tea, and took off her shoes.

It wasn't even five o'clock yet, and light was streaming through the window, but it felt like it was after midnight.

They drank tea and talked and then she asked him to kiss her, so he did, and then things started to get hot.

He hadn't had sex with a woman, that is to say a real woman rather than a doll, in almost five years. He had been pretty sure that he never would again, since his attraction had been solely for dolls. But he had to admit that Kimberly stirred something inside him.

"I want you," she said.

"I don't know."

"I do. I knew when I first saw you. I had a crazy intuition."

And she was right.

Afterwards she docked her iPhone on her stereo system and pressed play on her 'Best 90s songs EVER' playlist.

She served him some mint-chip ice cream and he told her that he was a photographer. He said that he worked for a magazine in New Jersey, but was careful not to say exactly what kind of magazine. If she knew that he worked for *Idollatry*, which was, essentially, a sex doll magazine, he felt it was pretty likely that she wouldn't have approved.

"You shouldn't be working in New Jersey," she said. "You should be working in Manhattan."

"Yeah, but I'm not."

"You could be. I'm sure you're a great photographer. I can tell. My dad runs *Inthuse*. I can get you a job there."

"*Inthuse?*"

"Yep."

"I don't know," Billy said.

"I do."

And she did.

4.

Inthuse was a men's style magazine with a circulation of 1.1 million. Their offices were in a building on 7th Avenue—a giant glass and steel opus of stiff luxury, suitable for both heterogametic sex and ostentatious suicide.

Billy rode the elevator up to the thirty-sixth floor and, after giving an elderly receptionist with pink hair his name, was led into an office the size of a basketball court. Kimberley's father was seated at a hand-carved Chinese table. The huge windows behind him showed a parade of Manhattan skyscrapers.

23

Mr. Courtney looked a little like Alan Alda. He wore an expensive suit but didn't have a tie on. He was drinking a cup of chai and harmonizing on Calm.com via his laptop.

Billy smiled and introduced himself.

"My daughter thinks you're pretty far out," Mr. Courtney said.

"Yeah."

"She asked me to give you a job."

"Yeah. She said I should come over and talk to you, but I'm not looking for any sort of special treatment or anything. I mean, it would be great to work at *Inthuse*, Mr. Courtney, but———"

"Call me Rick."

"Um, yeah. It would be great to work at *Inthuse*, Rick, but———"

Rick touched his mouth with his index finger and nodded his head and Billy did the same.

"You got a portfolio?"

"Yeah."

Billy took it out of his bag and plopped it on the table, but Mr. Courtney didn't even open it.

"Look Billy, let me be straightforward with you. I don't really care how good of a photographer you are or how bad. The important thing to me is that you make my daughter happy. That's what she told me—that you make her happy. She just came off a hard breakup with a real loser. Some guy from the Bronx who did nothing but smoke hashish all day and drink fresh goat's blood. You seem like a clean-cut, even-keeled young man, and Kimberley's fond of you—and that's all that matters."

"Yeah."

"You realize of course that I can't start you off in an executive position?"

"Yeah."

"Would a salary of ninety-two kay per annum scare you away?"

"No, sir, it wouldn't."

"Then see you tomorrow. Nine a.m. sharp."

5.

When Billy showed up the next morning, he was told he needed to go to the art department on the ninth floor and so that's where he went.

The department consisted of about a dozen boys and girls with ages ranging from their early twenties to early thirties, most of whom spoke in chipper voices, and a forty-year-old errand boy who had spent his youth listening to Ministry. One of the boys was wearing an Apliiq fleece cotton navy sweatshirt with a Prowler pocket. There was a refrigerator full of bottled water and Billy was told he could help himself.

He did.

A tall guy with short-cut red hair and glasses introduced himself.

"Hey, brother, I'm Todd Kovacs."

"I'm Billy Glandzk."

"So, I guess you need an assignment?"

"I guess so."

"We're doing an article on the fourteen best foods for summer virility and need some shots. . . . You know, buff guys eating watermelon, a well-dressed dude eating a swordfish taco, that sort of thing. Here's a list of shots that need to be taken. Just go down to the male model department on the sixth floor and they'll set you up."

"Swordfish makes you virile?"

"Omega-3 fatty acid, brother."

The shoot that day seemed to go pretty well. Everyone was super nice to Billy and bent over backwards to help him and make him feel at home. The male models they had for him were a sweet bunch of kids.

He was finished by three o'clock and then spent an hour editing the photos before handing them over to Todd.

"Awesome," Todd said. "Now I'm going to take you out for the best drink you've ever had in your life."

Billy was supposed to meet Kimberly for dinner, but that wasn't till 6:30, so he accepted.

Todd took Billy to a bar called Gil & Ross's, where a young Vietnamese man sat at a piano and played Dean Martin songs. Everything in the place was either black or white and to Billy it seemed pretty posh.

25

They sat down at a table and Todd ordered a couple of sidecars from a tall waitress.

When the drinks came, and Billy took a sip of his, he had to admit that it was the best drink he had ever had.

Todd smiled.

"Look, Billy," he said, "if you want to be a success at *Inthuse*, you need to learn to curate yourself."

"Curate myself?"

"The nails tell the tales."

Billy looked down at his fingernails. They weren't especially long, but they weren't short either. A few of them looked a little soiled.

"Shit," Billy said.

"Hey, don't get uptight, brother." Todd took a sip of his drink. "I'm going to open up. A few years ago I wasn't the man you see before you. I just hung out at home, smoked kizzle, and played video games. I belonged to a Satanic cult."

"Yeah?"

"That's right. I drew a lot, but most of it was just mermaid porn or characters from *The Lord of the Rings*. Then, for my 30th birthday, my aunt Mary Pat bought me a subscription to *Inthuse*. I started reading it, and realized that I was only living up to about a tenth of a percent of my potential. I joined a gym and STARTED CURATING MYSELF. I started focusing on function productivity and closing the emotional gap between me and my fellow humans. If I like someone, I tell them I love them."

"Even if you don't love them?"

"I do love them. I love everyone."

"That's sort of cool."

"It's important to give men hugs. The entire male species is like an extended family. I have a theory relating to evolution and how we, as males, emerged from tribal systems. We have to endure. We have to be both strong and fertile and develop overwhelming feelings of sacrificial love for each other and protect each other from the natural forces of attrition and predation that endanger the propagation of the species. It's necessary to give each other affirmation and advice."

"You want to give me advice?"

"Yes, I do. Your photography skills are awesome—I mean it, brother. I think you have the resources to really succeed at *Inthuse*. But you have to respect yourself and your manhood as a spiritual entity."

Billy realized that Todd was right. He had been letting himself go for too long. The next day, during lunch break, he went and got a manicure. It seemed to him that it was the best thirty-three dollars he had ever spent.

Later, when Kimberly saw his nails, she let out a sigh of pleasure.

"Nothing is a bigger turn-on for a girl than a guy with nice nails," she said.

That weekend, Kimberly told him that she thought they should move in together.

"You're spending most nights with me anyhow, and that way you wouldn't have to commute," she said. "I want to share my life with you."

Billy agreed and, a few days later, he gave notice on his apartment.

Most of what he owned he took to the Goodwill. He thought of selling his weird fiction collection on eBay, but decided it was more trouble than it was worth, so ended up sending the books via media mail to his nineteen-year-old cousin in New Mexico who was studying to be a hoist and winch operator.

Cleaning and clearing out his apartment was a big chore, but he found the experience to be liberating.

He took his three sex dolls and set them in front of his house with a cardboard sign that said 'Free'.

He looked at them with nostalgia.

"Well guys," he said in an emotional voice, "I guess you're on your own now. I won't forget you though."

He loaded a few more boxes into the back of his Suzuki Jimny, then got in and turned the key in the ignition.

As he was pulling away, he noticed a homeless man with a large beard dragging one of the dolls away.

A part of him felt that he had betrayed the dolls, after they had done so much for him, but it was a cruel world and he had no intention of letting anyone hold him back.

He cried a little as he drove through the Holland Tunnel into Manhattan.

6.

Billy took up fly-fishing, bought himself a handcrafted shotgun, and started reading parenting psychology books. Every morning he did fifty push-ups and fifty sit-ups, then showered and washed his hair with peppermint ginger shampoo, splashed on some Drakkar Noir and climbed into his Bluebuck briefs.

He felt full of energy and everyone at the office was impressed with him. He realized that confidence was a decision.

His relationship with Kimberly was like a butterfly alighting on a meadow violet. He let her see his sensitive side as often as possible and treated her like the quality woman she was. He was determined to be both realistic and flexible.

Kimberly had hinted that, should he propose marriage to her, she probably wouldn't say no. He wasn't sure if he loved her or not, but at the same time felt that this might be the real thing.

He and Kimberly usually made love for thirty minutes after dinner, and then watched *Game of Thrones* or streamed a film from Netflix. Sometimes she would fall asleep with her feet on his lap, and this made him feel tender towards her.

At work he was doing well. He liked his job and felt that he was getting somewhere. Everyone treated him with respect and he and Todd Kovaks had become friends.

"Great work on the 'Manliest Deodorant' story, brother," Todd said one Tuesday afternoon.

"Thanks."

"Hey, Cindy and I are having a little shindig at our place on Saturday and we'd be delighted if you and Kimberly could come."

Billy said they would be even more delighted to come and Todd gave him his address and told him to be there at around 6:00.

7.

On Saturday, when it was almost time to go, Kimberly said she wasn't feeling well.

"You're sick?"

"The magic of being a woman."

It had been quite a while since Billy had studied up on the female hormonal cycle, but he thought he understood.

"Right. Sure. I understand," he said.

"You go without me, honey."

"But I'd rather stay with you."

"And hurt Todd's feelings?"

"Yeah, I couldn't do that."

"Just make sure not to show up empty-handed."

He got in his Suzuki Jimny and Google-mapped the address Todd had given him, which was in Brooklyn, then turned the key in the ignition and headed off.

"Kimberley's right," he told himself. "I can't show up empty-handed."

There were some shops on his left, so he pulled over. He looked up at the signs. There was a Bloomingdales and a Sunglass Hut and a few others, but none of them seemed very promising. Then, across the street, he saw a place that called Pearl River Mart and he decided he might find something in there. There was potted bamboo, kung fu dragon fabric fans, and copper wind-chimes. He toyed with the idea of getting them a jar of bacon-flavored jelly beans, but realized that they might be offended, so finally decided on some scented votive candles.

Finding the apartment was easy enough. It was a brownstone in Park Slope, but Billy couldn't find a parking spot in front, so he had to park a couple of blocks away.

When he walked in, both Todd and Cindy gave him hugs. There was music playing and a fair number of people were already there. He didn't recognize the music, but if he could have used one word to describe it, it probably would have been oogenetic.

29

He handed Cindy the scented votive candles, which had been gift wrapped and she unwrapped them.

"Oh, cool, votive candles!" she said.

Todd smiled and led Billy to the bar.

It seemed that an actual bartender had been hired and he was impressed. The women were all drinking colorful cocktails and the men seemed to have resigned themselves to more serious drinks such as Scotch on the rocks or whisky and sodas.

Billy ordered an old fashioned and was told that the whisky was small batch. He sipped it and it tasted good.

"It's really good," he said.

There was a table full of appetizers, such as pickled asparagus, goat cheese, and garlic clam dip.

Billy took a piece of raw broccoli, dipped it in the garlic clam dip and munched on it. He wished Kimberley had come.

Everyone at the party was wearing nice clothes. The men all had short hair and a couple of them had beards. The women seemed to smile a lot. He noticed a young woman who wasn't smiling. She was standing apart by the bookshelf looking at a copy of *This Will Make You Smarter*. She was wearing a good vibes tie-dye blouse. Her hair had an arbitrary braid on one side.

Todd saw that Billy was staring at her.

"That's Tatum."

"Tatum?"

"She's Cindy's sister. Down for the weekend from Springfield. She's pretty outré."

Billy nodded his head. It didn't seem like a very nice thing to say, but he figured Todd knew her and he didn't so——

"Come on, brother," Todd said, "let me introduce you to someone cool."

He led him over to a man with adobe-colored hair who was wearing Armani Aqua Di Gio.

"Hey Nashton, I wanted you to meet a dear friend of mine, Billy Glandzk. He's one of the best photographers in New York."

"Lovely!"

Billy smiled uneasily and shook Nashton's hand.

"Nashton's a published poet," Todd said.

Nashton grinned. "Well, I'm really a veterinary epidemiologist, but I like to throw down a few lines of the old *vers libre* in my spare time."

Billy talked to Nashton for a while about Allen Ginsberg and animal carcasses and then somehow found himself in a conversation with a dark-haired man who said he was a probe test equipment technician.

"Your work's pretty interesting?"

"I'd say. I don't think I could ever stop working with semiconductor wafers. It's true that it's sort of a bachelor's job, spending so much time with the wafer probe equipment chuck—messing around with a vacuum wand or tweezers and dickering with the ohmmeter—but there's really something transcendental about it. It itches my brain, and that's what matters, isn't it?"

"Yeah, I guess so," Billy said. "Do you know where the restroom is?"

"You have to go pee?"

"Yeah."

"Well, I saw a few closed doors straight down that way. One of them's probably the toilet."

Billy walked in the indicated direction and did indeed find a few closed doors.

He opened one of them, but it wasn't to the bathroom. It was to one of the bedrooms. The room was filled with smoke. There was a single bed and Tatum was sitting cross-legged on it, holding a good-sized lit joint in her right hand.

"You can come in," he heard her say.

He went in and closed the door behind him. She was handing him the joint.

"I don't smoke," he said.

"It's just herb."

He noticed that she had very large eyes and he felt like her brain waves were reaching him through her eyes.

"What the hell," he thought.

He accepted the joint, took a long toke, held it deep in his lungs, and then exhaled. It was good pot, he could tell.

"That's pretty good weed," he said quietly.

"Yeah."

It was like meeting an old friend.

"I'm having strange vibrations on my lips," Tatum said.

"They look alright to me."

"You can't see vibrations."

He took another hit of the joint and considered what she said, thinking *Marky Mark and the Funky Bunch smaller and smaller parts of our reality as the wind moves across the globe, all the forces, all the building blocks, a rumble or a purr, or is there an evolutionary point to ejaculating?*

He passed the joint back to Tatum. She took a hit and, while exhaling, thought *life is all about frequency looking through my eyelids BOOM ancient Earth history, the Universal Time Matrix system atoms have formed as atoms this is so unexplainable to work with my anatomy I am not an organism I am every organism.*

Billy took a few more tokes and then decided he had probably had enough.

"I guess I should get back to the party," he said.

"Yeah," she replied.

"You coming?"

"Nah. I think I'll just stay in here and zone out. I feel out of place around Cindy and Todd's friends. You're cool, but——"

She didn't finish the sentence and Billy thought he understood what she meant.

He found the restroom, urinated, and then went and got another drink. He took a sip and looked around. Everyone seemed to be smiling at him. He didn't feel like socializing. He wished he had a giant jar of peanut butter. He remembered when he was thirteen and a kid named Aaron made fun of him at the lunch table. There were so many voices and the music seemed like a hammer driving a nail right between his eyes.

"I gotta split," he told himself.

He looked over and saw Todd in an animated conversation with a German prosthodontist, so decided not to say goodbye.

He swallowed off the rest of his drink and set the glass down on a bookshelf in front of a copy of *Here Comes Everybody: The Power of Organizing without Organizations*, then opened the door and went out.

He walked down the front steps. He took a deep breath. He was glad to be out of the party, but wished he had spent more time talking with Tatum. She seemed lonely, but he realized that it was also okay to be lonely.

The city seemed motionless. There were cars parked on the street, but it still seemed empty. He looked right and left but couldn't remember where he had parked his Suzuki Jimny. His iPhone couldn't tell him that. He was pretty sure it was to the right, so he started walking in that direction.

He found himself walking beneath a large brick building that seemed to go on forever. He thought he heard a sound coming from above, like the sound of someone sawing a board. He looked up, but didn't see anything. He stretched his neck back more and squinted his eyes, and just as he did this a peeled banana fell into his mouth.

Lazy

Butterscotch was a space scheduler at the University. He would compile lists of students who needed space for collaborative study or presentation practice. University faculty and staff would also often send him requests and, occasionally, even community groups would. He also had to make sure that rooms were cleaned before and after use and that everyone abided by room policies.

He had just got home from work and was tired because it had been a tough day and all he had had for lunch had been a cup of instant ramen. He had stopped by the Natural Foods CoOp and bought himself a couple of pork chops that he was going to cook and eat with brown rice.

He set down his bag and looked around the kitchen. It was a mess. All the pans and pots were dirty and there were no plates, bowls or cups to be seen. Even the forks and knives seemed to have disappeared.

"Fucking Toby," he said to himself.

He went to Toby's room and knocked on the door.

"Yeah?"

He opened the door.

Toby was hunched over in front of his computer. On the computer table there were dirty dishes piled up—bowls that still contained soggy cornflakes, cups brown around the rims from coffee, plates with pizza crusts and partially eaten quesadillas on them.

"You know," Butterscotch said, "if you use a dish, you should wash it afterwards."

Toby didn't reply.

"All the dishes are dirty," Butterscotch complained.

"Sorry," Toby said without looking up from his computer.

"I want you to do your share of the housework," Butterscotch said. "When you use a dish, wash it afterwards!"

"Okay," Toby said.

"So you're going to do the dishes?"

"Yeah."

Butterscotch left Toby's room and shut the door. He was both furious and hungry. He didn't think he should have to wash Toby's dirty dishes just so he could eat. He ended up driving to a nearby Chinese restaurant and getting a plate of shrimp chow mein, but it wasn't very good.

The next day when Butterscotch came home from work, he expected to see the dishes done, but they weren't. They were just stacked up on the kitchen counter beside the sink. Toby hadn't even put them in the sink to soak.

Butterscotch went to Toby's door. It was closed but he could hear him typing on his keyboard.

Butterscotch felt like opening the door and yelling him, but he didn't. He thought Toby should be taught a lesson. It wasn't fair that Toby expected him to do all the dishes.

The next day Butterscotch took an early lunch and came home from work at 11:00. He had stopped at the Koko Korean Restaurant on the way and got a bulgogi box to go.

He knew Toby would have classes then and wouldn't be home. He was right. Toby wasn't in his room.

Butterscotch went to the kitchen and got most of the dirty dishes—plates, bowls, cups, knives, forks and spoons, and brought them into Toby's room. He arranged them on Toby's unmade bed, making sure a lot of the forks and knives were pointing upwards, then went and ate his lunch.

That night he lay in his own bed reading Bookchin's *The Rise of Urbanization and the Decline of Citizenship*. He kept expecting Toby to burst into his room in anger, but he didn't.

The next morning when Butterscotch was headed out the door for work, Toby still hadn't left his room.

That day, Butterscotch again came home early at lunch time. On his way home, he had got a yardbird chicken sandwich to go from Fat Jack's. He set the sandwich down on the dining room table, but went to the kitchen to see if the dishes had been done before eating. The dishes were not there. He went to Toby's bedroom. The door was closed and he knocked but no one answered.

He went in.

Toby wasn't there.

Butterscotch went to the bed. A blanket had been pulled over the dishes but Toby hadn't bothered to move them. He could see spots of blood on the blanket and there was a pillow bunched up towards the top of the bed, so it was clear that Toby had slept on it. Butterscotch pulled the blanket back. A few of the bowls and plates were broken and some blood had seeped through to the sheets and mattress.

Some of the knives and forks had pierced through the blanket. It seemed strange to him that Toby hadn't complained.

"He's so lazy," Butterscotch said.

He folded Toby's blanket up, took it outside and threw it in the trash bin, then ate his yardbird chicken sandwich.

That evening, after work, he met his friend June Bug. They went to an Indian restaurant called Biryani Palace. Butterscotch ordered the heaven goat chops and June Bug got the egg masala. They had several large bottles of Taj Mahal beer with their meal and, afterwards, went to a bar called the China Blue and drank rum drinks until 11:30.

When Butterscotch got home, he was fairly drunk and went straight to bed. The next morning he woke up late, and had to rush to work in order to be on time.

When he came home from work that evening he looked in Toby's room. All the dishes were still there. But Toby was gone. Toby's computer was gone, as were his things.

Toby never came back.

Sex Life of a Bicycle Cop

1.

It was 2 p.m. on a Friday afternoon in late June, and though clouds were forming in the distance, around the parking lot of the Coronado Shopping Center, it was anything but cool. Waves of heat bounced off the pavement and sidewalks; a few pedestrians moped lazily along, wearing sandals and carrying bottles of water; the plants and trees in the landscaped areas drooped, hoping a crow would come along so they could be fanned by its wings.

Ricky Fishback, dressed in dark blue shorts and a light blue polo shirt with the police department logo on the breast, rode past the Secreto Cantina and, through the large open windows, could hear the television. It sounded like they were watching some sort of sporting event. He glanced over and could make out the outlines of a few men hunched over the bar drinking beers or Long Island iced teas. He wished that he wasn't on duty and could go in and join them, order a beer and maybe a plate of hot wings and watch whatever they were watching. He nodded to a young man smoking a hand-rolled cigarette in front of the lounge and then rode on.

His weekday route consisted of the area around the Coronado Shopping Center, the scenic city park and its exercise pathways, and the downtown district. He was, however, sometimes called into other areas if there was any sort of emergency need. But this seldom happened.

He had been on duty since nine that morning, but had only issued two tickets—one to a guy wearing an old Bernie Sanders T-shirt for jaywalking and another to a biker who he had caught blowing through a red light. The jaywalking ticket he probably wouldn't have even issued if the guy hadn't been wearing that T-shirt, but Ricky hated Communism with a confused and fuzzy passion, so the ticket was as much for that as the misdemeanor. The basic quota the department gave him was five tickets a day and he had set himself a personal goal of double that—a figure he usually met. But today was just slow.

He figured he would cruise by the 'handitrap' to see if he could make a quick sale, as it was his go-to spot when he needed to pad his quota. The 'handitrap' was a parking space in front of an 'Italian' restaurant with an old, extremely faded handicap designated stencil on its tarmac. The truth was that Ricky wasn't even sure if it was still meant to be a handicap designated space, as the markings seemed left over from a previous era, but he had issued quite a few tickets there and so far hadn't heard anyone complain.

Sure enough, there was a vehicle parked over the invisible wheelchair. It was a silver 2002 Nissan XTerra with a 'Keep Honking, I'm Reloading' bumper sticker. Just under its left rear tire, an extremely vague, faded stencil of a person in a wheelchair could be made out if one looked hard enough.

He got off his bicycle, took out his ticket tab and stood with legs wide apart as he began to write a ticket.

"Hey!"

Ricky looked over. A short individual with a bandana, a Jägermeister T-shirt, a significant amount of untended facial hair, and tattoos over his muscular arms was standing near him.

"Hey, that's my vehicle!" the man said.

"Yeah, you're parked illegally."

"Illegally?"

"You're not handicapped are you?"

"Huh?"

"You're parked in a handicap spot," Ricky said, pointing to the vague white markings beneath the rear tire.

"You've gotta be fucking kidding me!?!"

"No, sir."

"Are you writing me a ticket?"

"Sure am."

"Un-fucking-believable!"

"Maybe you're not familiar with this neighborhood, but around here no one who isn't handicapped parks here."

Ricky handed him the ticket he had just penned.

"Here you go," he said.

"Two hundred and fifty dollars? That's total bullshit. I just stopped for five seconds so I could run in and give my girlfriend who works in Andiamo's her cell phone that she forgot."

"Sorry."

"You're not even a real fucking cop."

"Sir . . ."

"You're a fucking bicycle cop. You can't write me a ticket."

Ricky was just about to reach for the can of pepper spray on his belt when he felt himself being lifted off the ground and the next moment he was back on the ground and the world was dark and blurry around him.

2.

When he got home he opened an IPA, took two Tylenols and sat down on the couch. His back hurt like hell. He lay down on the couch and put his feet on a cushion, but that didn't make him feel any better.

His iPhone rang. It was Dan Chavez, one of his buddies on the force.

"Hey," Ricky said, answering.

"Hey, you okay? I heard you got into an altercation."

"Yeah. My back is all screwed up. I think I'm going to call a chiropractor."

"Fuck that shit. You need acupuncture."

"Acupuncture?"

"You need to go see Dr. Lo. That dude's a fucking wizard. I'll give you the number. Just call up and tell them that Dan Chavez sent you."

41

After Ricky got off the phone, he polished off his beer, lay back and closed his eyes.

"Being a bike cop sure isn't for sissies," he thought.

Ricky had been on bicycle patrol for the past two years. It had all started when Dan Chavez had told him how often he scored due to the patrol.

"You meet women on bicycle patrol?" Ricky had asked.

"Are you fucking kidding me? Just look at the stats. Do you know how many contacts, on average, a patrol car has with citizens in a given hour?"

Ricky said that, no, he did not know.

"Three point three. And a bicycle cop? Guess. Seven point fucking seven. Up close and personal. In the zone. You need to be on the patrol, dude."

And so Ricky had applied for the bicycle patrol. He went through a four-day course of intensive training and specialized instruction that covered patrol procedures, tactics, night operations, emergency dismounts, basic bike maintenance and on-the-road repairs. He swerved around traffic cones, rolled down flights of stairs, did bike-specific live-fire exercises and then was given a black and white Trek patrol bicycle, a pair of shorts, and set loose on the world.

And Chavez had been right. During the first year of his patrol, Ricky had got more pussy than in the previous twenty-seven years of his life. His OkCupid account became a wasteland. His Tinder app gathered thick layers of dust. Cruising through the malls and downtown parking lots, he came into contact with countless women. Young ladies would ask him directions and three minutes later they would be contacts on his iPhone. He noticed that, when he was in bike cop uniform, women wouldn't pull back if he touched them—even if they were complete strangers. He had made it a point of honor that, if he met a cute woman, he would make a pass at her within thirty seconds. Routine interactions would quickly escalate to thick sexual chemistry. And it wasn't just the expected types that he would score with—it was all sorts of women, from alt chicks to independent freaks. Single mothers in search of blended orgasms, twenty-two year old blondes who had just broken up with their boyfriends, upbeat brunettes with east-west breasts, chest-heavy redheads in pink tank-tops, Goth chicks with tattoos on their thighs, mysterious women with large lips, sex-crazed librarians, party girls and nymphomaniacs, alpha females efficient in the bedroom, tomboys with tear-drop tits, free spirited rebels who liked to scratch, hopeful romantics, soul-mate seekers up for a fling, perky-bottomed nerd girls, stunners and sexual goddesses.

But as it says in *The Book of Changes*, "When the sun has reached the meridian altitude, it begins to decline. When the moon has become full, it begins to weaken. The interaction of heaven and earth is now vigorous and abundant, now boring and flimsy, growing and diminishing according to the seasons."

One big transformation on the patrol had occurred when Chavez had been caught having sex with an HB8 on the seat of his bicycle. The whole thing had been caught on surveillance video. Fortunately the incident had been hushed up and never made its way to YouTube, but Chavez had been taken off patrol and given a desk job back at headquarters.

And not long after that, for Ricky, things mysteriously had begun to slow down. When a woman asked him directions, he forgot to give her his flashing smile and ask her where she was from or tell her how much he loved the color of her eyes. He would get women's phone numbers and then fail to follow through, or take them out on dates but fail to force things to escalate. Instead of sweaty nights amidst needy whimpers and tangled sheets, things would end with a peck on the cheek or even a hug or a handshake. Had he lost his lust for life? The thirty-second rule turned into two minutes, the two minutes into five. . . . And then he started missing opportunities—lots of them.

He wasn't sure what was going on. He started making himself kale smoothies, taking damiana leaf capsules, and eating more fish, but nothing seemed to help. He felt flat.

He googled around and discovered that excessive time in the bicycle saddle could hinder blood flow to the genitals and decided that must have been the cause of it. He had thought about giving up his patrol, but then was worried that, instead of putting him on a car patrol, they would put him behind a desk, like Chavez. The latter had put on twenty pounds in the last year and didn't look so good. Ricky had decided to stick it out.

3.

He wasn't sure what he had expected, but when he walked into Dr. Lo's office he was agreeably impressed. A blonde, rather good-looking woman sat behind the counter in the waiting room. She smiled at him and asked him for his insurance card and had him fill out a short questionnaire. Afterwards he sat and waited for a few minutes, flipping through a book titled *Chinese Art Treasures: A Selected Group of Objects from the Chinese National Palace Museum and the Chinese National Museum, Taichung, Taiwan.*

Dr. Lo was a lean, pleasant-looking man with easy manners and a confident gaze. He led Ricky back to his office where he had him sit down on a small chair opposite him. Ricky told him that he had hurt his back and that his friend, Dan Chavez, had told him that he, Dr. Lo, might be able to help.

The doctor smiled at him affably and asked him to stick out his tongue. Dr. Lo nodded his head then took his right wrist and felt his pulse. He scribbled something down on a sheet of paper.

"How is it?" Ricky asked.

"Little weak. How is your . . ."

"My . . . ?"

"Energy."

"You mean . . . ?"

"Yes, that's right. How is it?"

Ricky frowned and shook his head. "Not so good," he said.

"Okay, don't worry. We'll fix you up."

"My back?"

"That too."

A minute later Ricky was standing in a small, simply furnished room. There was a single chair, an acupuncture bed, a space heater, and on the wall a five-color standard chart of meridians and acupuncture points.

Dr. Lo told him to strip down to his underwear and socks and he'd be back in a few minutes. Ricky did and he was.

Ricky lay down on his stomach on the bed, placing his face in the cushioned hole.

When he was a child he had been afraid of needles and would always scream in their presence. But he wasn't a child anymore, and didn't scream.

Dr. Lo started out with a needle in the shoulder. He asked Ricky how it felt and Ricky said fine. Then the doctor started jabbing them everywhere: all over his back, on the top of his head, behind his ears, on his calves and on the outer sides of his arms. Some of the needles stung slightly, but Ricky found that things seemed to be going pretty well.

"Just take it easy," Dr. Lo said.

He cut off the lights and left the room. Ricky wondered how long he would have to lie there. Dr. Lo hadn't said.

He could feel the needles beginning to burn in his back. He felt like getting up and leaving, but clearly that wouldn't be a simple matter with eighteen or twenty needles sticking out of him. Plus, he didn't want to act like a pussy.

As he lay there in the dark, all sorts of thoughts flashed through his mind. He remembered when he had been a child of five, how attracted he had been to Minnie Mouse and seeing her in her red and white polka dotted skirt would have feelings of emergent lust. He recalled many years later, when he had first started trying to date in a serious way and how almost all the girls he liked would either next him or friendzone him. He spent most of his time alone, ignoring his potential, coming off as needy, lifting five-pound weights in his bedroom and watching *Friends*. Then one day, while waiting for a haircut in a barber shop, he had started reading an article in *Man's World* magazine about how to score with chicks— an article that lifted the wool from his eyes and, while the barber was trimming the thick thatch of hair on his head, he came to the revelation that women were made to be gamed. That afternoon, he had put in for a full subscription of *Man's World*, and from then on took the magazine as LAW. In the furnace of his soul he began to forge new habits. Control the situation. Avoid victim mentality. Don't be ruled by fleeting emotions. Understand the world you live in. Adapt. Then, finally, women started spontaneously touching him—not just unattractive women, but attractive women as well—not just HB6s, but HB7s and 8s too, but he hadn't had enough INTERACTION needed to be where he could be seen. The first rule: GET HER FUCKING CONTACT INFO! And women started giving him the green light anywhere and everywhere. Must BANG! SEAL

THE DEAL! Daisy Duck is walking towards him, shaking her tail SHE ISN'T WEARING PANTIES JUST WHITE FEATHERS would spend two hundred bucks on a venison dinner I have many problems to make my life worthwhile DON'T JUST EYE FUCK HER for some of that shrimp and king crab IT'S THE BICYCLE STUPID you have a gun practiced some unarmed combat put all the time in the gym burgeoning don't be a FUCKING doormat take advantage of her moral shortcomings ENERGY flowing left where are my dark-wash jeans?

Suddenly the light went on. Ricky blinked rapidly. He had forgotten where he was.

"Okay? Great," Dr. Lo said as he removed the needles. "I'll give you some special herb tonics and you come back next week."

4.

The 9th of July was another hot day. Riding through the streets and parking lots, Ricky felt like he was touring a series of Samsung ovens and ranges. He had been drinking water all day but decided he needed something cool and refreshing, so he went into Starbucks to get himself a handcrafted Frappuccino® beverage. The place was almost empty. There was a girl at the counter he had never seen before. She had long, sandy-blonde hair and somewhat thick features and was, Ricky decided, a clear-cut HB6.

Three minutes later, she was handing him his Frappuccino® and Ricky pulled out his wallet to pay.

"It's on the house," she said.

"Yeah?"

"You're a police officer, aren't you?" she said with a smile.

Ricky nodded his head. He was a police officer, but he had never been given a free Frappuccino® or any other type of coffee for it before. He had heard that the Southside car patrols got as much free coffee and donuts they wanted over at the Dunkin' Donuts on Central, but he had been in Starbucks a hundred times in uniform and had always been charged full price—if not more.

Ricky started to walk away with his Frappuccino®, and then suddenly turned and told the woman that she had a cute smile.

And she did.

Her name was Tina. They met that evening at Felipe's for tacos. She had changed and was wearing a white summer dress and a skimpy army-green jacket that she probably couldn't have buttoned up if she had wanted to. He observed that she had a tiny gold cross around her neck. He hadn't noticed it before, but she might have been wearing it. Seeing her in the dress, which really complimented her figure, he decided she was an HB8 rather than an HB6, but the cross worried him a little.

"Normally I wouldn't go out for tacos with a guy I don't really know," she told him as they sat eating their food.

"Yeah, so why did you?"

"Because you're a cop."

"That makes a difference?"

"Sure it does. It means that you're probably not a creep."

Afterwards he asked her if she wanted to go back to his place to look at his keychain collection, and she said that she did, so she followed him in her corsa-blue Kia and he led her inside. He opened a couple of beers and served them with slices of lime. It didn't take long before he was kissing her and feeling her body.

"I don't usually fool around," she told him.

"Neither do I."

"Really?"

"Yeah, it's been a long time since I've been with a woman."

"Okay. Wow."

He took her hand in his and held it. She smiled. A moment later he was putting his mouth around hers and making a non-equivocal move. She seemed hesitant at first, but was soon more excited than he was. Ricky guessed that she probably hadn't been with many men, but that was just fine with him.

5.

The next day, while he was on patrol, he got a text from her.

> It was nice being with
> you. I hope you feel the
> same.

He replied:

> Yeah it was great :-)

A minute later he got another text from her:

> Are you thinking of me?

He replied:

> Yup.

Five minutes later:

> Should we meet
> tonight?

But he didn't reply. He had just spotted a young woman with rich black hair and athletic cantaloupe breasts—an HB9. She was sitting on the curb talking on her cell phone and crying and Ricky figured she was probably going through a break-up and that he should help her.

And he did.

The next day he received a few more texts from Tina and the day after that a few more, and a voice message that he didn't listen to, and then they stopped.

"I guess she took the hint," Ricky thought.

6.

The next month was a whirlwind of untamed lust. Any woman walking through the Coronado Shopping Center parking lot would have Ricky ride up next to her. If they weren't at least an HB6 he'd just nod, smile, and ride on. But any HB6 or higher who was by herself or with another chick, he'd hit on, and more often than not get her contact info. He slept with two sisters who were on vacation from Germany. They even cooked lasagna for him and showed him how to kiss the German way. After that it was a mad fling with a brown-haired vegan who managed an olive oil and honey shop, and then a long and sharp series of one night stands—the daughter of a janitor, a forty-two year old ex-HB9, a college student who wore purple lipstick and had breast implants, a gymnast who was obsessed with elephants, a small Asian woman with a strong Texan accent.

Ricky felt like a million dollars. He went to see Dr. Lo regularly and drank his herbal tonics as if they were nectar from heaven. He had his game back.

7.

On Friday, the 5th of August, Ricky met Dan Chavez at the Buffalo Wild Wings sports bar. Dan certainly had put on some weight in the last year and Ricky noticed that his hairline seemed to be retreating, even though he was only thirty years old. He wasn't quite at Norwood 3, but it was apparent that he would get there before long.

They got five orders of wings between the two of them, three traditional, and two boneless, as well as an order of fried pickles. Ricky ordered a beer and Dan a watermelon mojito.

"So how is your back?" Dan asked.

"Totally better. You were right, that Dr. Lo is a wizard."

"Told you. He give you the tonics?"

"Yeah. Been taking them twice daily."

"Fuck yeah," Dan said, and reached for his drink.

"And how is the, um, desk job?"

"It's like someone just pushed the slo-mo button on me. Not getting exercise. Put on weight. And my sex life . . ."

"Yeah?"

"Yeah, it feels like chicks just see right through me. No eye-contact. No smiles. I have a really tough time amusing them and they don't seem keen on amusing me. I used to be able to just kick back and pussy would just sort of magically fall in my lap. I was going through a mattress every six months. Now I go out and I see these chicks passing me up for low-quality sperm."

"So, you're not getting ANYTHING?"

"No, I get a few low-value lays. Last week I scored with this thirty-five year old single mother without an ass. I got an HB4 on for tomorrow, but . . ."

"Dude."

"Yeah."

Ricky felt his phone go off. He looked at it. It was a missed call from Tina, which he ignored. She had already tried to call him three times the same day, and received the same treatment. Ricky figured that she had a hankering, but he wasn't really interested.

"Whassup?" Dan asked.

"It's this chick I banged a month or so back. She's been blowing up my phone."

Dan was nibbling on a wing. "The main thing you have to do is fucking keep your autonomy," he said. "Don't lose that backbone, because it's all you have. Live carelessly. Be a fucking Caesar, the fucking captain of your fate. Pass on the low-hanging fruit and stay hydrated. Purge your mind of non-sexual intent and gain a four digit n-count. This is the true path to manhood."

"Yeah, that's all cool," Ricky said, "but what about you?"

"Fuck, brah, I don't know. I guess I gotta start lifting again. Shed a few pounds. Hop on Minoxidil and get a hair transplant. Get out of this fucking tear-stained dress I've been wearing. But that desk job just tires the shit out of me."

Dan reached for a slice of fried pickle and sadly slipped it into his mouth.

8.

The next day was gorgeous. The sky was a cerulean blue, spotted here and there with cut-out clouds that looked like they had been taken from a Warner Brother's cartoon. On Saturdays, Ricky had to patrol the Farmers' Market, which was just about five hundred meters north of the Coronado Shopping Center. The main thing he had to do was remind people with dogs that their animal was not allowed in the market unless, by chance, it was a seeing eye dog.

It was a big day for Ricky because there was a lot more quarry about than usual—HBs everywhere. It was true that, at the Farmers' Market, the majority of them were libs and alt types, but he was an adult and knew how to separate politics from the bedroom. He noticed that his score ratio was a good bit lower with them than with, say, Tea Party babes or cowchicks, but he still managed to make a significant amount of contacts . . . and once contact was made they were often much more willing to put out.

He had been hovering around the market since 8:30 that morning and it was now almost noon, so he decided he should do a quick tour of the district. He drifted towards the Coronado Shopping Center, wondering vaguely what he should have for lunch. There was a Nathan's a few blocks away, but the clientele there was mostly uggoes and washed-up women— and he was tempted to just settle for a Kava juice and leave it at that—but he also needed protein—he should probably stock up on whey protein—a bunch of zinc—fish oil—amino acid replenishment—grape seed extract—a tailgate dog at Nathan's would go down pretty easy though——

"Excuse me, officer!"

Ricky's nose suddenly detected the sweet scent of Eau So Sexy

Parfum.

A woman was waving at him and he rolled to a stop in front of her.

She was about five-foot-two and one hundred and ten pounds, with reddish brown hair with balayage highlights. She was wearing skinny jeans in snow wash with extreme shredded rips. She had a tattoo of a dreamcatcher on her upper left arm. At first Ricky mistook her for an HB7, but as his eyes roamed up and down her hourglass-shaped body, a masterpiece of mounds and gullies, he realized that she was definitely an HB9. Right away he wanted to touch her.

"Excuse me, officer," she said.

"What can I do for you, ma'am?"

"Do you know where Andiamo's is?"

"The Italian restaurant?"

"Yeah, I'm supposed to meet a girlfriend there for lunch."

Ricky was used to giving people directions. It was one of his favorite parts about his job. With a few easy motions of his hand and gentle but firm words he explained how to get to the restaurant, which was quite near.

"Oh, wow, thanks so much," she said. But she didn't go right away. She was still standing there smiling at him. Her eyes, which were like those of a fawn, shone and her mouth, which was the color of hot sauce, looked inviting. Something began to stir inside Ricky.

"Hey, um, by the way, my name's Ricky. Ricky Fishback."

"I'm Briana," she said. "Briana Lynn."

Ricky noticed that she had a wedding ring on.

"I'd ask you for your phone number," he said with a smile, "but it looks like you're taken."

"I'm separated," she said.

"Yeah?"

"Yeah, I kicked the bastard out."

"So you're getting a divorce?"

"Yup, just waiting for the papers to be finalized."

"Right on."

Ricky looked down at her breasts. Her nipples were poking out and seemed to be sending him secret signals.

"I'm going to close with this little critter tonight," he told himself and immediately asked her if she would be interested in meeting him later, after he got off work.

And she was.

9.

He had wanted their first date to escalate quickly, so he took her out for laser tag. The quick movements and competitive friction excited them both and the next thing he knew they were back at his place peeling each others' clothes off.

"Oh, Ricky," she gasped.

He tried to say something, but couldn't. She had sealed off his mouth with her own and her lance-like tongue seemed to be seeking out his heart, which was pounding furiously.

The next morning, when he woke up, she was already gone—and he was already craving her again. He promised himself that he wouldn't call her or text her for a few days, but by noon he had already sent her a text asking if she could come over again that night—and she seemed as keen as he for further adventure.

Briana was just about the wildest woman Ricky had ever known. Normally he would sleep with a woman once, or maybe five or six times at most, and then move on. But the more he slept with Briana, the more he wanted to. She was like an acrobat in bed. She did things he never knew existed—was an expert in the arts of amour, a roving gazelle eager to give and receive pleasure—clinging to him devouring in darkness grabbing at the gun sex nature in bruises love play sweet perversion. Scratching in unusual postures and anarchic frenzy. Stinking of arousal and crescendos of spasms impetuous meridians ascending. Sometimes in bed she would call him 'captain' or 'boss' before her voice broke down in inarticulate sounds and this enlivened Ricky greatly. She was insatiable.

They would move from the bedroom, to the shower, to the kitchen, together riding a tidal wave of lust, their pretzel-like passion unifying them in rhythmic panting.

The cumulus cloud is billowing

Feathery crane hoists its wings
Hungry lion bellows while
Dew drops adhere in an essential purple
Mounds of bubbles
Joining their delicate essences
In seething foam as
The traveler penetrates deep
Into the dark and misty mountains
On drumbeat wounds
Mating amidst thunder
And the brazen needs
Of scratching leeches

They would always meet over at his place. She said it was better that way.

"The divorce papers aren't finalized yet," she said, "and, for all I know, that dick-face Sébastien is spying on me. I like to be at your place. We can do whatever we want."

And they did.

10.

The morning of the first of September was on the cool side and Ricky was a bit groggy. Briana had hardly let him sleep at all the night before, straining and draining him as if he had been the last man on earth.

As he was biking by Starbucks, a strong desire for the unique leathery flavor of their coffee struck him.

"But Tina . . . ?" he wondered.

It had been quite a while since he had seen her and he knew that the turnover at Starbucks was high anyhow. He doubted she was still working there—or even if she was that it would be her shift.

But he was mistaken. She and another woman, a short, dumpy-looking girl who seemed unreasonably cheerful, were behind the counter. Tina noticed Ricky right away, so he didn't have a chance to beat a retreat. He approached the counter.

"Hey."

"Hi, Ricky."

"I'll have a caffè misto and, um, a cranberry orange scone, I guess."

The short, dumpy-looking girl had overheard the order and began making the caffè misto while Tina got Ricky his scone.

"Don't worry," she said when Ricky took out his wallet to pay.

"You sure?"

"Ricky," she said, "I need to talk to you."

"Okay."

Tina told the short, dumpy-looking girl she was going to take a five-minute break. She walked outside with Ricky.

Ricky took a sip of his coffee.

"I'm pregnant, Ricky."

He smiled. He wasn't sure if he should congratulate her or not.

"You're the father, Ricky."

"Huh?"

"Yeah. You're the only man I've been with in three years."

"Oh," Ricky said.

"When we were together I felt a deep, penetrating happiness. I was so sorry that you didn't feel the same, Ricky."

"I—well—I had a lot of fun too."

"Did you?"

"Sure, but . . ."

"What are you going to do, Ricky?"

"I'll take you to the clinic. I don't mind paying for it."

"What do you mean?"

"To get rid of it."

"Oh, Ricky! No! No, no, no! I'm a Christian. All of God's creatures have a right to life."

"Um, yeah, okay."

"Don't you want to know what God might have next for us? . . . I've been praying for weeks that I would see you, Ricky—that you would text or call me. I feel that you're a good man, even though maybe sometimes you have a hard time admitting it to yourself."

Ricky was silent. He took a bite of his cranberry orange scone without even tasting it.

"Maybe we can talk more when I get off work?" Tina said.

"Yeah, maybe."

11.

The 8th of September was busy as hell. That morning, at 9:05, he had ticketed an eleven-year-old vandal for writing his name on a park bench. Then had busted a guy in a parking lot washing car windows and, not twenty minutes later, caught a man in baggy pants drinking from an open container. He then threatened a bearded gentleman holding a 'DISABLED VET PLEASE HELP' sign with arrest for panhandling and ticketed a young man standing outside a bookstore and wearing summit-white Nike Air Maxes for loitering.

By noon he was well beyond his daily quota and treated himself to a tailgate dog and an order of crinkle cut French fries at Nathan's.

He then turned his attention to the city park, cruising along the exercise pathways, checking out the female joggers and mentally rating them. It was usually around the skate park that he ran into the most trouble. The kids there were always stoned on one thing or another and, sure enough, as Ricky approached, he caught a distinctive odor. There were five or six kids in wool caps and jeans standing around with their skateboards passing a marijuana cigarette back and forth between them, but hadn't noticed him yet. That was the beauty of being on a bike—total stealth.

He verbally reprimanded them, lectured them on the dangers of drug use, confiscated a bag of weed. He then biked around for a bit, advised a man in a 2003 Ford Mustang at the park's edge that he had his car stereo turned up too loud, and headed towards the Coronado Shopping Center.

After riding past the Secreto Cantina, he decided it was time for a Red Bull break.

He stopped, got off his bike, took a Red Bull energy drink out of his fanny pack and opened it. While vitalizing his body and mind with the Red Bull energy drink, he started checking his iPhone. He had a few e-mails from vendors of Cialis and Viagra, one from his sister who worked at a Tommy Hilfiger outlet, and——

"Excuse me . . ."

Ricky looked up from his phone.

A man wearing a white Oxford popover with a partial button front placket was standing in front of him.

He was about six-foot-two with a chiseled jaw and long brown hair. He looked like he must have been in his late thirties, but was obviously in good shape. Judging from his arms, which stretched out the cotton fabric of his popover, he clearly did a lot of lifting.

"Excuse me . . ."

"Yeah?"

"Is your name Ricky?"

"I'm officer Rick Fishback. Why?"

"My wife is seeing a cop named Ricky."

"Probably quite a few guys named Ricky on the force."

"He's a bicycle cop."

"Well . . . there are a bunch of us."

"Named Ricky?"

The man was grinning, but not in a friendly way.

"I don't know," Ricky said. "I, um . . ."

"My wife and I have been going through some tough times and some asshole named Ricky's been fucking her while I'm not looking. I love her and she loves me and I don't need some douchey pig on a bike fucking things up."

"I'm not sure I know what you're talking about."

"I'm Sébastien, Ricky. I'm her fucking husband. I check her phone. I pay the bill, so I have a right to know who she's texting with. Some fake fucking cop in shorts who thinks he knows how to tantric massage my lady."

"Sir . . ."

Sébastien was clenching his fists and Ricky was determined not to have a repeat of the handitrap incident back in June.

"Stay the fuck away from Briana, Ricky—you got that? Stay—the—fuck—"

The man was now yelling. Ricky instinctively reached for his pepper spray; protecting freedom crushing crimson berry wind ripping tree the sound of the stag get off your fucking hooves. The man was on the ground screaming, covering his eyes with his hands. Then he started waving his right hand around in front of him and Ricky kicked him in the ribs.

"Stop it!" the man screamed. "Stop it! This fucking cop's assaulting me! Help! Help!!!"

Ricky looked around. A few people were standing in the distance, staring. Then, not too far away, he noticed a young man pointing his iPhone at him.

"I got it. I got the whole thing on video!"

12.

Ricky was more than a little nervous when he walked into Captain Pogonowski's office. The latter was sitting at an Ameriwood Westmont Collection executive desk in resort cherry and gazing at his Kindle Paperwhite. His somewhat round face was marked with severe dimples which made him seem like he was always either smiling or about to.

"Hey, Ricky," the captain said.

"Hey."

Captain Pogonowski invited Ricky to sit down, and he did.

"I guess you know why I wanted to talk to you."

Ricky said that, yes, he could guess why the captain wanted to talk to him.

"Someone got part of it on video. You're on YouTube, Ricky. It's got over fifteen thousand views and sixty comments."

"Yeah, well, I'm sorry about that. I didn't know I was being filmed."

"Everyone's got an iPhone, Ricky. You should know that. A superior officer should never forget that danger may come in the form of video footage. I'm afraid I'm going to have to take you off the patrol. This is the second incident in three months."

Ricky felt like someone had just socked him in the throat.

"But neither of these was my fault," he said in a taut voice.

"I'm not saying they were, Ricky. But, you know, it isn't just that . . ."

"What do you mean?"

"Well, you also have gotten a sort of reputation. A reputation that isn't good for the bike patrol. If you want to date girls, do it the right way . . . go on OkCupid."

"But . . ."

"Yeah, I know it's rough, Ricky, but that's where it's at. I'm going to have to rein you in. You're going to be put on the administrative unit."

"A desk officer?"

"Yup, Ricky. That's just how things are going to have to play out. You'll be one of the guys holding down the fort."

Ricky left Captain Pogonowski's office.

In the distance he saw Dan Chavez walking by holding a take-away bag from Arby's, but the latter didn't notice him. He was in profile and Ricky could see his vanishing hairline and his belly sagging over his belt buckle.

Ricky went to the water cooler, got himself a cup of water, and drank it. Officer Bibiana Veskler, a senior clerk typist, came up to the cooler to fill her blue Intak hydration bottle with water. She was four-foot-eleven, one hundred and sixty-three pounds and wore Burt's Bees Suede Splash lipstick.

"Hey, Ricky," she said, as she leaned over to fill her bottle with water.

"Hey."

"Why so down?"

"I'm off the bike patrol. Desk duty."

"So we'll be seeing more of you around here."

"I guess so."

"Feel like you're in a rubber cell?"

"Yeah, kind of. Feeling really down. It's like life is . . ."

"Leaving you behind?"

"Yeah."

"I know the feeling. You should see my iridologist. She's fantastic."

"Iridologist?"

"She'll look in your eyes and help you out."

Ricky wandered outside to his car. It was just about lunch time and he thought he might run over to Felipe's and get himself a few tacos. They had amazing shredded beef tacos and had a four-tacos-for-five-bucks lunch special. The last time he had been there was with Tina. He had had fun with Tina that night. She had been the one who had taken him out of his dry spell.

Ricky unlocked the door of his car and got in, taking his iPhone out of his pocket as he did so. He tapped on the Messages app, and there were messages, lots of them. Messages from women he had dumped, and those he had not yet screwed—from HB6s 7s and 8s—from cop-curious college students to sex-jaded check-out clerks—from super bangable semi-sluts to hungry cougars begging to be tamed. Then he saw one from the week before, from Tina, that he hadn't read. He opened it.

> **I'm off work. Want to meet so we can talk?**

He hadn't seen it or answered it.
"I'm such a dick," he said to himself.
Then he typed in a message and sent it. It said:

> **Can we meet tonight to talk? I will take you out for dinner. Andiamo's. Do you still want to see me?**

And, in fact, she did.

The New Normal

1.

Miss Shimazaki, at seventy-five, was the youngest member of the Daikanyama Senior Center English Club. To call her fascinating would have been an exaggeration; to call her effete, less so. For, just as new-fallen snow is a rather attractive sight, old snow has a tendency to fill one with both pity and remorse—though, strangely, the same cannot be said of old trees, which are looked on with at once awe and veneration—but if Miss Shimazaki had been a tree, it would have been an old plum tree that, though it gave off few flowers and less fruit, gave off blooms of great beauty, and fruit that, though not as abundant as that bestowed by a younger tree, was certainly not without its sweetness.

"If I were a fish," Mr. Hidari said, "I would swim in ocean!"

"*The* ocean," Justin Isis (may his head be blessed by a thousand stars!) corrected.

"If I were clam, I would love pearl!" Mrs. Rusu said.

Justin nodded his head. He didn't have the energy or desire to correct her.

Miss Shimazaki did it for him.

"If I were *a* clam, I would love *pearls*," she said.

Justin sort of wished that they were all clams, since he instinctively felt

63

more connected to things lower on the evolutionary scale, random ethers rotating around Hedean rocks, amniote vertebrates or silicoflagellates riding wild, aborted frenzies that rest beneath rusty bushes.

Teaching English was not his favorite thing to do, but he hadn't had a modeling job in over six months and most of the random ways he tried to earn money—such as support testing for avionics, being a volunteer tour guide, writing dōjinshi, part time theme park work, selling Chinese Rolexes on the street, freelance eyebrow tinting, distributing fliers in Ebisu, polishing trombones, selling Expensive Japanese Mango (Egg of the Sun) via Skype chat, preordering movie tickets, selling illegal organ meat, reading artistic poetry at birthday parties, photographing exotic pets, interviewing 'Australian' women in Oji park—never ended up panning out.

After the lesson, he went to a bar called Jetrobot and ordered a Hofbräu Original. His iPhone rang. He didn't recognize the number.

"Hello?"

"Is this Taeka?"

"No, it's not."

"Is Taeka there?"

"No, she isn't. You call this number every fucking day. It isn't her phone number. Now fuck off!"

He then wandered around for a few hours, sauntering meaninglessly through a number of youth-oriented boutiques before finally buying himself a bottle of Bravas hair liquid at a shop on Takeshita Street.

"It's very kitschy," the salesgirl said.

"Pretty hit or miss," he thought as he walked out.

He went to a nearby convenience store and bought a hotdog. He was just opening up a sachet of mustard to put on it when the Sherwood Forest text tone of his iPhone went off.

The message was from Miss Shimazaki. It read:

Private lesson???

2.

He had never thought of Miss Shimazaki as especially wealthy, but it was clear by her house that she must have been. The carpet was so thick that he was worried he would sink and have to be rescued by someone with specialized knowledge and skills. A bamboo basket by Jan Lee stood on a curly koa pedestal. There was a chrome Ron Arad chair up against the wall and a giant alligator leather sofa placed in front of a Fredrikson Stallard coffee table.

They sat down on the sofa and a maid named Sharan served them edible fruit and martinis.

"So," Justin asked, "do you want to just do conversation or were you thinking of an, um, more grammar-orientated lesson?"

"Mr. Justin, let me be frank with you," Miss Shimazaki said in Japanese. "I did not invite you here for an English lesson."

"No?"

"No. I realize it is not very lady-like to be so blunt—but I am enormously attracted to you."

"I'm sorry."

She raised her eyebrows and smiled.

"That is a very cruel remark," she said.

Justin frowned. He hadn't meant to be cruel, but the words had just come out like that. He took a swallow of his martini and wondered if he should apologize for apologizing or not, but decided that he had better not, as he might be misunderstood.

"Look Miss Shimazaki, I like you, I really do."

"And I like you. A woman's heart never lies you know."

"Never?"

"Don't slap me!"

Justin bit his lower lip. He had had students come on to him before and it was always an awkward situation. The last time had been the twenty-two year old wife of a yakuza gang boss and he had had to politely refuse. He sometimes wished he had been born a hunchback or with a face like Mick Mars.

He took a sip of his drink, sighed, and raised his eyes. He noticed that there was, at the far side of the room, a large framed photograph hanging on the wall. Something about it looked familiar. He got up and, carrying his drink with him, went over to look.

"That is my late husband."

His heart raced suddenly, slowed down, and raced again. He recognized the features.

"Your husband was Masato Shimazaki?"

"Yes."

The tone of her voice was almost embarrassed.

Justin took a deep breath. In Australia, as a teenager, he had worshiped Masato Shimazaki, founder of ShimaCorp, one of the world's most important sellers of clothing, cologne and skincare products. He would endlessly watch a VHS tape he had acquired through mail order called *Designer Shimazaki Moves and Talks*—an exquisitely rare biopic narrated by Dick Cavett—and it was, in fact, Masato Shimazaki who had inspired Justin to move to Japan in the first place.

"So cool!" Justin said in English.

"Turn on the heat?" Miss Shimazaki said in the same language.

Justin granted her a smile and then returned to the language of Mitchisuna no Haha, Kafū, Anrakuan.

"No, the temperature in here is perfect. I was just saying that I find it really wonderful that your husband was Masato Shimazaki."

"He was a great designer, but living with him was not always mandarin ducks and spring rain. Yet I really should not complain, since he did leave me the business."

"The business?"

"Yes, ShimaCorp."

"ShimaCorp?"

"ShimaCorp high-style clothing."

"Wait, you mean you OWN ShimaCorp?"

Miss Shimazaki looked thoughtful for a moment.

"I don't exactly own it," she said, "but I am the president and principal shareholder."

3.

Justin's apartment consisted of a single tiny room in Ikebukuro. There was no furniture in the place—unless a futon mattress on the floor could be called furniture. The last light bulb had burned out a few days before and he hadn't got around to replacing it yet, so the only source of light was his iPhone. He padded to the refrigerator and opened it. Inside was a jar of Blue Flag peanut butter, a bag of Pasco 'Soft and Fluffy' bread, and nine OneCups.

He opened a OneCup and, by the light of his iPhone, made himself a peanut butter sandwich, using a three-inch black plastic comb to spread the peanut butter on the bread since he didn't have any silverware.

He sat down on the futon mattress and, while munching on the peanut butter sandwich and drinking the OneCup, reasoned as follows:

"Miss Shimazaki is too old for me, sure, but that is only because, whenever reality is confronted by common sense, contradictions arise. But, if empirical processes are used, it becomes evident that she must have been hot when she was younger. If Masato Shimazaki married her, she must have qualified as being VERY hot. But whether she was hot or not, is too old or not—these points are subordinate to the question at hand, which arises due to MY BET WITH RICH, which has evoked in me certain perceptions in regard to the external world. Miss Shimazaki could directly correlate with the functional dependence of me winning said bet."

He finished off his peanut butter sandwich and washed it down with the last swallows of his OneCup.

"Fuck it," he then said aloud.

He picked up his iPhone and sent Miss Shimazaki a text message:

Want to marry me?

He then got up, went to the refrigerator and got out another OneCup.

67

Just as he was returning to the futon, the text tone on his iPhone sounded. He looked. It was a reply from Miss Shimazaki:

Yes.

4.

The marriage went off without a great deal of pomp. Afterwards she took him shopping and bought him a Rick Owens faun messiah caban coat in raisins red with an off-center zipper.

He thanked her and they hugged in public.

"I guess you get free English lessons now," he said and laughed.

"You are like a calamus leaf coming close to my nipple," she replied.

"Oh, Miss Shimazaki!"

"I am Mrs. Justin!"

"Yeah?"

"But call me Keiko, baby . . ."

Justin's transition as CEO of ShimaCorp was like a pebble caressed by the waters of a limpid stream. He was given a huge office with a bocote desk, an antique snow cone machine, and a rope swing that hung from the ceiling.

His secretary, Natsuo, a eunuch from Kagoshima, treated him like an orphan would treat his adoptive father on homecoming day.

"Just anything. Anything you want. You tell me. Snacks?"

"So I can do whatever I want?"

"Excuse me?"

"I'm the boss, so I can do whatever I want, right?"

"That's correct, Sir, though . . ."

"Though?"

"Though—yes, though. Though, technically speaking, any major decisions should be run by the Board. But seeing as how Miss Shimazaki——"

"Mrs. Justin."

Natsuo blushed.

"Yes, seeing how Mrs. Justin is your—well—of course she is! Seeing how your wife is such an *important person* at ShimaCorp . . ."

5.

He met Mika at Bar High Five for drinks. She was wearing a raspberry tanktop, a black Himitsu Kessya skirt and white Jeffrey Campbell shoes. A few months earlier, Justin had thought about asking her to go steady with him, but then he saw her spit in the street, and decided not to. She had also told him that she could only have a romantic relationship with a convivial guy, and he didn't consider himself to be one.

She ordered an elaborate drink made with Noilly Prat vermouth, orange bitters, and professional-grade ice. He ordered a glass of red wine.

"Isn't she maybe a little old?" Mika asked him.

"Well, yeah, but that's not why I married her."

"I know why you married her, J-bon. It is for her money."

"You really think I would marry a woman for her money?"

"Yes, I do."

He shook his head. Mika took a sip of her drink and smiled.

"Listen Mikachi," Justin said, "I don't think you really understand what kind of a person I am."

"I think I do."

"What do you think?"

Mika pursed her lips together by way of reply.

Justin bobbed his head and then spoke:

"I know I seem like a fun-loving guy, Mikachi, but I'm not. I was with this Chinese girl a few months ago whose name was Chunhua. We were at her apartment holding hands and she started hyperventilating. I just held her and stroked her hair and told her what an amazing person she was. About a month ago I was at Lawson getting pork buns and saw a guy drop a ten thousand yen note."

"And you returned it to him?"

"No, when he walked away I picked it up. I texted my friend Rich and we went out and had drinks together."

"That's bad."

"Why do you say that?"

"Maybe it was the man's last money? Maybe he really needed it?"

"Umm, but, like—I've seen you steal from homeless people and even children, and you're always shoplifting."

"That's different. I'm a girl." She took a sip of her drink. "The point is that I was right about you."

"Right?"

"That you got married to that old woman for her money."

"No, that's what I'm trying to explain. Rich and I went out for drinks."

"Where did you go?"

"Tafia."

"Isn't that where the bartender has hair like Billy Ray Cyrus?"

"Yeah, but he's cool."

"Maybe for guys he is, ha ha!"

"Umm, right. . . . Anyhow, Rich and I were getting pretty drunk and we started talking about success. He said he thought the key to success was being nice to people and I told him that I didn't think he would succeed like that and he told me I didn't know what I was talking about and if there was anyone who wouldn't succeed it was me."

"Oh!"

"Yeah. I told him that I would succeed, give me a year, and he told me he thought it would take me more than a year and, if I were honest with myself, would probably never happen unless I started getting into transportation and logistics."

"Rich sounds like he is smart."

"Yeah, I dunno."

"So you wanted to get into transportation and logistics?"

"No, that's just a foxhole. The important thing is the bet."

"You gambled?"

"No, I made a bet with Rich that, in a year's time, I would either be successful, kill myself, or move back to Australia."

"What is so bad about Australia?"

Justin smiled indulgently. He was just about to tell her a few disconcerting facts about Australia, when his iPhone rang.

"Hello?"

"Hi."

"Umm, yeah?

"Who is this?"

"You're calling me, so you should know who I am."

"Taeka?"

"No."

"I'm calling for Taeka."

Justin hung up. He looked at his glass and noticed it was empty, then saw that Mika had also finished her drink. He signaled to the bartender, whose hair was like Stalin's at age twenty-three, for another round.

"So?" Mika asked him.

"So it's not about money, it's about success."

6.

He started a line of home objects called J-good. He took up bowling and had sex with fourteen gravure idols on the same day. He had all the furniture in his office reupholstered in pistachio-green silk. His costume creations were featured in *Boon*. He formed a mania for pottery. He met Hikaru a.k.a. Piichan, the singer from Black Diamond and Shizuoka Event Project Team, one night at a bar and they formed a blood-pact in the restroom. He was accepted into the Chambre syndicale de la haute couture and, three days later, bought Flaubert's penis at auction. He was supposed to meet his friend Rich to play tennis at the New Otani Golden Spa, but the latter ended up drinking a few too many OneCups and falling asleep in a public park, so Justin found himself standing alone in the middle of a tennis court wearing a pair of orange TravisMathew shorts and a gecko-green Asics shirt; a week after this, however, he was walking along Meiji-Dori with Rich when two men on a motorcycle drove by and the man on the back had a

bow and arrow and shot an arrow into Rich's thigh. He wrote an article on experimental fashion techniques that was published in *Marie Claire* and he experienced external reality
like some lean orgasm
the blinking
blinking
blinking
pixilated
car friction sandy stipules
like love of skyscraper
TALL
flesh
such muscle standing
in Tokyo tension
a diet of sex behind stairs
limber butterfly
winging **WHOOSH**
WHOOSH
through
voltage
hovering snail
sliming over
VOLTAGE
Justin ranging freely
weight permanently the party at Alfredo
ZOOM
flesh
in karaoke café
continue to send infinite
ZANG
sex behind shrines
YES
do as not I function
the last visit of the waveform of news-feeds.

7.

Justin had had a long day at work. He had been negotiating terms for a new six-pocket vest with a manufacturer in Guangdong and felt brain-weary. He came in, set down his briefcase, and began to unfasten his Salvatore Ferragamo tie.

Just as he was kicking off his shoes, Sharan, the maid, rushed in with a gin fizz and handed it to him.

He let his tongue be lapped by the botanical flavor and nodded his approval.

Sharan made an expression like a baby finch being offered its first worm.

"Shall I serve you dinner in the dining room?" she asked.

"Has Ms. Keiko already eaten?"

"Yes, she ate some pineapple cake. But I'm sure you need something more muscular for your supper."

"Yeah, just have Maurice fry me up a donkey liver with onions and I'll eat it while watching TV."

"Do we have any donkey liver?"

"We'd better."

Justin went to the fun room, sat down on the couch and, picking up the remote, snapped on the 152-inch plasma display panel TV. He toggled through the channels until he got to MTV. A video by Babymetal was playing and he watched this while sipping on his gin fizz.

Miss Shimazaki came in. Though it was only 8 p.m. she already had her nightgown on.

She looked at Justin and frowned. He muted the volume on the television and looked up at her.

"Justin, honey, I'm very upset with you," she said.

"Umm, why?"

"You don't know why?"

"If it's because I ate the last bag of Hello Pandas, then I'm sorry. I meant to buy more but spaced it out."

"No, the Hello Pandas are not important."

73

"Thanks."

"I spent today with accountant Ito."

"Yeah?"

"Yes. We were looking over the books and saw a strange expenditure for ¥132,515,957. I contacted all the Board Members, but no one knew anything about it, so I asked Natsuo and he said that you had spent the money on a penis."

"Yeah, Flaubert's penis."

"If you do things like this you will ruin the business!"

"But haven't sales gone up since I took over?"

"That is a minor point. This thing you bought——"

"Flaubert's penis."

"IT IS VERY UNHYGIENIC!"

"It's a prestige item and will help our corporate identity."

"IT HAS TO BE SOLD!"

"No."

"Yes!"

"No."

"YES!"

"No."

"YES!"

"NO!"

That night Keiko insisted that Justin sleep in the guest room, which was okay with him. He lay on the guest bed browsing the web via his iPhone but didn't feel tired enough to go to sleep, so ended up calling Rich and asking him if he wanted to go out for drinks. Rich did, so they met at the Tiberius bar.

"How is the thigh?" Justin asked him.

"Ninety percent."

"Ninety percent?"

"It's mostly better. I guess an arrow wound is not as big of a deal as most people think. There's not much hydrostatic shock. In a couple more weeks I'm going to go into training."

There were not many people in the bar, but at one table they noticed two young women sitting together, so they went over and introduced themselves. The women were Filipino and turned out to be sisters whose names were Tessa and Rose. They both worked as special assistants to DFA

Undersecretary for International Economic Relations Laura Q. Del Rosario and they weren't averse to letting Justin and Rich sit with them.

Tessa asked Justin what he did.

"I'm a magician," he said.

"Oh, can you do a trick for us?"

"Sure. I'll make this glass of beer disappear."

He did, but nobody was very impressed.

"I don't think you're really a magician," Rose said.

"Yeah? Watch, I'll make it so you can't take off your clothes."

"Go ahead and try."

Justin asked the bartender, who had tousledcurlyedgyshag hair, for salt. He made a mystical diagram on the table and muttered some words that no one recognized.

"Now try to take off your blouse."

She couldn't and, in fact, was unable to undress for quite some time.

8.

The next day he didn't arrive at work until eleven. He felt a little uneasy in the head and decided it must have been the gin fizz he had drunk the night before.

"Mr. Justin, you're late!" Natsuo said.

"Yeah."

"Everyone's waiting for you!"

"Huh?"

"I called you many times and sent texts and left messages!!!"

Justin looked at his iPhone. It was on mute. There were eighteen missed calls, around four hundred unread texts and numerous unheard messages.

"So what's it all about?" he asked, flicking the mute switch off.

"Miss Shimazaki called a board meeting and everyone is waiting for you."

"Yeah?"

"The penis, Sir."

When Justin walked into the boardroom it felt like he was walking into an icebox. The warmest thing in the room was a giant painting of Masato Shimazaki by Chuck Close.

Seated around a 900 cm mahogany conference table that was shaped like a boat were Miss Shimazaki, President, and the six Executive Vice Presidents:

1. **Kazuo Kamei**. Mr. Kamei provides leadership as brand champion at ShimaCorp and actively serves on ShimaCorp's Strategy Committee on cardigan and footwear matters. An industry veteran with more than 40 years of experience, Kamei has held senior executive positions within the fashion industry with recognized brands such as Sumon Ranch, South Star Undergarments International, and X-Boy. He is the recipient of the 2012 Underwear Sales and Marketing Association International (USMAI) Underwear Marketer of the Year Award and was named one of the Top 25 Most Extraordinary Minds in Underwear Sales and Marketing. He lives in Shibuya-ku and enjoys warm winds and moonlit stars.

2. **Kenji Tanabe**. Mr. Tanabe is the former Vice President of Public Affairs and Communications for Shirtcity Co., Ltd., and has over 30 years' experience in diverse corporate functions, including a 7-year assignment to NYC during the 1990s with Emporium Merchant International Corporation. His strength lies in the creation of overall communication strategies and key message content. He also has a strong interest in promoting socially and environmentally sustainable corporate business practices. He lives in Shibuya-ku and appreciates Italian food and jazz.

3. **Takaaki Igarashi**. The pursuit of excellence has been the hallmark of Mr. Igarashi's career. He is a recognized authority in lounge suits and jackets, and has been interviewed extensively on television, radio and print, and is also a popular industry speaker at business seminars and conferences in Japan, Oman and India. He knows how to use a hammer and indulges in golfing, fishing, hiking, diving, skiing, bowling and yukigassen. He lives in Shibuya-ku and teaches karate at an orphanage in his spare time.

4. **Yukata Sato**. Mr. Sato has a passion for applying fashion to improve human life and to share that vision with the world. Prior to joining ShimaCorp, Mr. Kobayashi served as General Manager at the Snoopy Town Shop in Yokohama. Prior to this, Mr. Sato served as an executive at a US manufacturer as Head of Corporate Planning and as Managing Director at a private equity fund. Prior to this, Mr. Sato was Chief Representative in London, Director General for Business Development (M&A) Department and New Business Department at Krisp Clothing. Mr. Kobayashi has earned an MBA from the Cornell University Johnson Graduate School of Management and a Bachelor's degree from the Bunka Fashion College. He enjoys Johnny Depp movies and lives in Shibuya-ku.

5. **Toru Ueki**. Mr. Ueki is a legend and a leader in the world of fashion hosiery. His vision has helped reshape concepts of hosiery throughout the industry. Mr. Ueki served as Vice Chairman of Sock World from 2001-2002, after serving as President and COO of the Azknit Knitting Group, starting in 1988. Under his leadership, the Group was awarded the Chen Tini Hosiery Sales Award in both 1992 and 1999. Mr. Ueki has also served on several boards. Mr. Ueki has authored several books, *The Technicalities and Practices of Hosiery Turnarounds* (co-author, July 2004, Economic Spinning Research Institute), *The Practice of Fashion Knitting* (author and editor, May 2011, Kinzai Institute for Socks and Textiles). He lives in Shibuya-ku and enjoys conversing with interesting human beings while sipping special wine, eating strawberries and sitting beneath the summer sun.

6. **Fumio Bannai**. A man is best described by his passions. For Mr. Bannai, his life-long passion has been men's skin care products. Internationally recognized as the foremost authority on men's skin care products, his three decades of accomplishments reveal a man whose unique vision has shaped the skin care product world like no other. His success in marketing and promoting men's skin care products has prompted the media to dub him the 'Skin Care Products Guru'. Mr. Bannai currently serves as a member of the Lotion Cleanser Rehabilitation Committee at the Center for the Promotion of Facial Cleansers. Mr. Bannai has earned a Bachelor's degree from the Faculty of Commerce at Waseda University. He dislikes people who are disrespectful or arrogant. His interests are marine diving and ham radio. He lives in Shibuya-ku.

Vice President Kazuo Kamei stood up and, after making the sign of antinomical fallacy, spoke:

"Mr. Justin, for many years now we at ShimaCorp have persevered in enhancing our global image. The single most important strength of the Company is an organic system that maximizes our ability to create clothing content that neither offends nor acts as a disrupter of dreams. You, by purchasing the penis of Flaubert, in a probable attempt at making our brand seem more 'muscular', have in fact undermined this seamless coordination."

Vice President Toru Ueki rose to his feet and, after making the gesture of cognizing individual faults, spoke:

"It is probable that Mr. Justin was, when purchasing said penis, unaware of the corporate attitude regarding penises in general and French penises specifically. But a lack of knowledge does not necessitate forgiveness, as set down in Article 7 of the Rules."

Vice President Takaaki Igarashi stood up abruptly, stared before him in silence for a moment, made the sign of judgment by re-judgment, and then uttered the following words:

"The Company values our shareholders, our business partners, and our customers. Corporate governance is an important factor in improving long-term stable corporate value. The Company recognizes the importance of our public and social responsibilities. The purchase of Flaubert's penis goes against Company policies and traditions."

Vice President Yukata Sato rose to his feet, made the gesture of the negation of supersensuous objects, and spoke:

"Mr. Justin, by purchasing Flaubert's penis without authorization or consultation of the Board, you have violated Articles 7, 12, and 18, the latter Article specifically stating that decisions that have an impact on the interests of shareholders, customers and employees, shall be reported, without exception, to the Board."

Vice President Toru Ueki leaped up, made the gesture of the static universality of things replaced by a similarity of action, and then spoke:

"The wind blows chrysanthemum flowers through the sky. When profits are up, one must guard one's product line. Early barley never can hear the admonitions of the cicada."

Vice President Fumio Bannai heaved himself out of his chair, made the gesture of *a priori* pure intuition, and then spoke:

"We hereby announce that Mr. Isis Justin will step down as Chief Executive Officer of ShimaCorp effective immediately and be made junior member of the claims department. He will there, upon request, fetch water from the water cooler for senior members as well as procure senior members such things as rare Chinese herbs, random snack foods, and the contact details of tall South American women."

Justin felt like a rooster waking from a nap a loser to wine-and-dine a vertical firefly the winner a fan in court of the base board office like a thin cloth stretched to the fan-a-fan of wind in the Milky Way and was just then going to give his opinion on the matter when his iPhone rang.

He answered it.

"Hello?" he said.

There was silence on the other end.

"Hello?" he repeated. "Who is this?"

"Taeka?"

9.

Mika hadn't seen Justin in some time and was glad when she received a text message asking her if she wanted to have lunch. He told her to meet him in Minato, at the Wakame Elementary School, in front of room 12. When she got there, the door was open, so she stood there and looked in.

Justin was standing in front of a chalkboard in a room full of children between the ages of six and eight.

"Like banana pizza!" one boy shouted.

Justin put on his angry face.

"Who likes banana pizza?" he asked.

"I like banana pizza!" a smart girl shouted.

"Banana pizza!"

"Banana pizza!"

"I like banana pizza!"

Just then the school bell rang and all the children bounced out of their seats and skipped and grinned their way past Mika.

"Seems like you have a lot of cute kids," she said to Justin.

"Yeah," he replied.

They walked down some steps and out of the building.

It was a beautiful spring day. A few clouds that looked like steamed rice sat in the sky. An old man leaned on his cane and looked up, forgetting his age.

"That's great that you got a job teaching at a real school!" Mika said.

"It's just temporary until the spell I cast on Miss Tiaga, the real teacher, wears off."

They went to McDonald's. Mika ordered the shrimp fireo sandwich and an iced hazelnut latte. Justin ordered a biggumakku and a chocolate mac sheikh and was reaching for his wallet to pay when Mika stopped him.

"No, let me!"

"But I invited you."

"Yes," she said waving a little purse with lady bugs on it in front of him, "but I got this from one of your students, ha ha!"

They found a table and sat down.

"If you have to cast spells on people just to find temp work," Mika said, "maybe you didn't succeed after all."

"Yeah."

Mika laughed and then took a very small bite of her shrimp fireo sandwich.

"What's the funny?" Justin asked.

"Well, you didn't go back to Australia or kill yourself."

"Actually, I did go back to Australia for Christmas to visit my family. And I did try to kill myself."

"Oh?"

"Yeah."

"You ate sleeping pills?"

"No, a llama fetus."

"What's a llama fetus?"

Justin looked thoughtful for a moment while he was chewing on a bite of his burger.

"The fetus of a llama,'" he explained. "I know a guy in Bolivia who sent me one. I was pretty sure if I ate it, it would kill me, but it didn't."

"That's good."

"Yeah."

After finishing their meal they went outside. There was the sound of traffic, but it seemed very distant. Justin noticed something pink near his foot. He thought it was a convolvulus blossom, but it turned out to be a candy wrapper.

"I have to go clean my apartment," Mika said.

"Yeah?"

"Yes. I have things lying . . . all over the place."

"Okay."

Mika smiled.

"Thanks for asking me to meet you for lunch," she said. "I had a lot of fun."

"Me too. I haven't had so much fun in a long time."

The Amazing House

Let me start by saying I am a horrible person, not horrible in the sense that I kill things, but because I say mean things about people all the time, and when I say all the time, I really mean it—all the time, from the moment I wake up in the cool alarm-clock 7 a.m. dawn until when I go to bed at night in my J.Crew dreamy cotton pajamas, I keep saying bad things and, yeah, some of my friends declare that it is because I have a self-esteem issue, but that's because they are so much less than hot and I am so much more and they want to crunch me like a corn chip, but not happening, and, no, I have no plans to undergo the hardships of therapy, would much rather just force myself to love people like they deserve to be loved and break out of this never-ending cycle of negativity, but when I really think about it, this very self-awareness makes me BETTER than, like, ninety-nine percent of the people I know, and yeah, I can be cordial and most people think I am super sweet and, anyhow, I was going to say, or not say but mention, that I was at the gym on the stairclimber with a sweater tied around my waist and was listening to an acoustic mix on my iPhone and there was this guy next to me on the treadmill in business clothes and he kept looking at me but, like OMG, he was about ten years too old and was balding and the smell coming from him reminded me of one of those Arby's pepper bacon sandwiches, so I looked at him and told him that he wasn't allowed to wear a suit in the gym and that men who eat pepper are a major turn off and that he should probably cut back on the hash browns, but he just smiled and started, like, asking if I was from Finland or something, so I went up to the sundeck and changed to a salsa mix and started doing some sexy stretches and there was no one there so I just thought that maybe I should relax, so I lay down on the sundeck even though it wasn't sunny and, anyhow, next thing I know that same guy is there and he sits down on a chair and starts drinking a Rockstar Lime Freeze and asking me what my name is and I told him that my name was fuck off and I felt like cancelling my gym membership and left and—yeah, just pay attention and I'll explain how about two months later I was visiting my cousin Coco in Topanga Canyon and she's all right and sort of cute, but one of those girls who probably need a period tracking app because she's probably slept with, like, a million guys, and she's so annoying that to be around her I have to use a calm app, and she took me out to a party, not a friend of hers house, but a friend of a friend's, but actually it was her friend's co-worker's friend's house, and her friend was named Wren who had a super cringeworthy shrill voice, and her friend's co-worker was Jason and he was gay and was wearing Fry James lace-up boots, and when we got to the party we had to park, like, a hundred miles away because there were cars all up and down the street, and then when we were finally there, I was, like, WOW, because the house was AMAZING, not some shitty McMansion, but a beautiful multi-level HOME with a chateau-like feel and a painting that I swear was by Damian Hirst on the wall and some really cool pop music was playing that sounded like the Black Eyed Peas but wasn't the Black Eyed Peas, was *even better* than the Black Eyed Peas and there was all kinds of food including a table full of French cheeses and Tuscan crackers and I wondered who the caterer was because there was a Korean guy with long hair making sushi hand rolls and a full bar with a guy without his shirt on mixing drinks and I got a green apple martini and my cousin Coco got a sex in the driveway and Wren got a hot 'n' sassy with extra jalapeño and Jason got a Manhattan and then he, Jason, said that he should introduce us to the host whose name was Fabio, who was a friend, but not *that kind of friend* and he walked us up to Fabio who was surrounded by about six hot bodies who were all trying to dance with him and hold his hand and when we walked up I knew I had seen him before but wasn't sure where and he asked me if I remembered him and then I realized it was the same guy who had been on the treadmill, but he had been balding and wearing a suit in a gym and he was still wearing a suit but a NICER one and he wasn't balding so he must have been taking Minoxidil or something and I thought how weird is that, here this guy seems SUPER COOL but at the gym he seemed like a real dick and then he went off to change the music saying it was time for his 'Ultimate Party Songs' playlist and I told Wren and Coco and Jason my story of the gym and then Wren said, yeah, here he seemed really cool, but, actually, she had seen him in Costco the month before with a shopping cart full of large pieces of random meat and he was wearing droopy sweatpants and a lumberjack shirt and she had noticed his troublesome skin and in the cereal section he had started trying to talk to her saying that he liked Nature's Path Organic Pumpkin Seed Flax Plus Granola and she was all I could care less what you like as she reached for the Lucky Charms and then she had seen him again out front as she was getting her Polish sausage and he asked her for her number and she ended up having to eat her Polish in her car, but the weird thing was that there, in his house, she said that his skin looked fine and she wondered what kind of skin product he had started using, because when she had seen him at Costco he looked like crap and she had thought she would rather date herself than a jerk like that and then new music started playing that sounded like Era Istrefi, but wasn't Era Istrefi, but some singer none of us could identify and was, like, ten times better than Era Istrefi and the lyrics were in ENGLISH and we looked over and Fabio was dancing, totally hot, kind of like he was Drake but *way* smoother than Drake, and then my cousin Coco confessed that she too had seen Fabio before when she was walking her dog Falcon in the park and he had pet her dog and asked what its name was and tried to hit on her and she had totally iced him out because he was too old, too bald and DEFINITELY had bad skin and we were all looking at Fabio as he was doing his moves with all these hot chicks in tight dresses trying to press up near him and doing all sorts of sexy moves and me and Coco and Wren all sighed at the same time and then Jason asked us if we wanted to go outside and take a puff and I don't smoke but Coco and Wren wanted to so I followed them because I didn't want to be left standing there by myself and so we were outside and they were smoking this awful-smelling WEED and Coco said that she would have given Fabio her number in the park if she had known he was so cool and Wren agreed and said she should have too and not eaten her Polish in the car and I said that, yeah, maybe I should have been a little bit nicer to him at the gym and Jason nodded his head and exhaled out this giant cloud of smoke and said, that is because you are all super judgmental and each of you had a chance to hang out with Fabio who is the coolest guy I know but you all blew it, and then Jason walked into the house and the house disappeared and there was nothing there and Coco and me and Wren were just standing out on the street alone and it was cold.

The Divinity Student

With Quentin S. Crisp

Monday

He awoke at 2 a.m.—an hour later than usual, but he had stayed up too late the evening before, reading Volume 156 of the *Patrologiae cursus completus*, which is to say the volume containing those most fascinating letters of Manuel Chrysoloras as well as the *Chronicon maius* of Georgius Sphrantzes.

"I awake in darkness," he thought, "but dawn shall before long form over the mountains, and the wind shall come and blow my troubled thoughts away."

He arose from bed, lit a fourteen-inch taper that had been donated to him by Canon Michael Brockie, of the Church of Our Most Holy Redeemer & St. Thomas More, which he stuck in a five-inch glass taper-holder with a silvered mercury finish, and, after performing his morning ablutions, donned a 100% wool habit with a stiff, pointed hood.

He knelt before a small wooden crucifix that hung on an otherwise bare wall and said matins prayers. He then carried the taper to the kitchen, made himself a cup of tea, went to his desk, set the cup of tea down on the left-hand side of the desk, the taper down on the right, and sat down himself, in a straight-backed wooden chair that had been with him since the beginning.

The hand-written letter from the previous day was there, and he looked it over with little satisfaction.

"No, I will have to begin afresh," he said, in a somewhat leaden voice.

He set a piece of clean, crème-colored paper before him, dipped his hand-blown glass pen in a bottle of lawyers' ink, and, in a fit of exultant inspiration, composed the following missive:

Dear Mr. Patric,

I am sure you will do me the justice to admit that, since I have occupied my present residence, I have been most punctual in paying you the rent monthly, as it has fallen due. Circumstances, however, over which I have no control, have conspired just at this moment to cause me several disappointments in money matters, to my great temporary inconvenience. Thus situated, I am induced, with the greatest reluctance, to request that you will be kind enough to permit the month's rent which is now due to you, to stand over until the beginning of next month, at which time you may rely on receiving the amount of the two months together. Your compliance with this request will oblige, sir, your obedient servant,

Mark Samuels

He read the letter over once, nodded his head in satisfaction and then recalled those immortal lines of Cercidas:

Why then doth the balancer even
Never unto me incline?

This was however a question for which he had no logical answer, and so he answered himself with a logical sigh. He opened the drawer of his desk and took out an envelope and a packet of stamps. He folded the letter, inserted it into the envelope, licked the envelope and sealed it and then addressed it and affixed a stamp to the upper right-hand corner.

He looked at the clock. It was almost 4 a.m. If he wished to go for a morning walk before the streets became dense with the offspring of Eve, he would have to do it now.

He took off his wool habit and put on a pair of jeans, a long-sleeved checkered cotton shirt, diamond socks and a pair of Clark's desert boots. He slipped into a mocha overcoat, set a light-weight, burgundy-colored wool fedora on his head, then opened his desk drawer and took out a fifteen-inch Circassians-Muhajir Kinjal dagger, which he installed in the right-hand pocket of the coat, while into the left he slipped a sack of Vape Stick brand rolling tobacco, a box of matches, and a BLU Samba Jr. handset with built-in FM radio receiver, address book, text messaging and office tools.

Thus equipped, he left his apartment, which was situated above Kiplings Restaurant and Bar, on Hill Street.

Outside the air was cool and thick with a mouse-like fog. He rolled a fag, stuck it in his mouth, and lighted it.

He began a leisurely march up North Hill and, after about three hundred yards, came to a letter box, extracted the letter from his pocket, popped it in the box, and then continued on to Church Road, swung right and went on until he came to Archway Road, which, at that hour, was all but abandoned.

He struck east, toward the Boogaloo.

Two-storey brick buildings stood on either side which, he imagined, had in bygone days been the resort for merry roysterers and quaint-faced ladies. One of the buildings someone had painted dark green. He wondered what sort of person lived there now. Undoubtedly some magician or tool grinder—some fellow who, in the blank of the morning snored easily, dreaming of flowers and hay.

The green color of the building reminded him of moss, but the building itself was, as fact would have it, completely moss-free.

He often wished that more moss would grow on the sidewalks and walls. He imagined that, if there were fewer pedestrians and motorists and people scrubbing at surfaces, there would be a great deal of moss everywhere.

He crossed Southwood Lane and continued on.

The buildings here were Edwardian, the bottom storeys taken up by shops—Tonton Nails, Oriental Café, British Spirals & Castings.

Moving past these, he came to a building which he saw as rather curious.

It was old—seemed to be one of the oldest, if not the oldest, on the street. The top windows were of oddly-tinted glass. It was of red brick with stone dressings. Down the walls a few drain pipes made their way. They had once been painted black, but the paint had mostly peeled off, revealing the color of raw tin.

He noticed a light on in the basement window and then, gazing up, saw that there was a sign that read:

Credentes Baking Co.

"What a peculiar name," he said aloud.

He had read recently, in an article in the *Catholic Herald*, about how odd bakeries were popping up all over London, in the most unexpected places—in old powerhouses, dismantled cash and carries, and debtor's prisons. He had even heard of a bakery that had recently opened in the cloakroom at Victoria Station.

When he had been a young man just starting out on the adventure of life, he had been advised by a certain poet of great repute to become a baker.

"People can do without many things," the poet had said, "but they cannot do without bread."

Indeed, if he had heeded the man's advice, and become a baker rather than a composer of not-so-ordinary tales, he, undoubtedly, would not at that moment have been shy of rent money.

His nostrils, oblivious to conceptual thought but not to subtle essence, found themselves dilating in a most pronounced manner—as nostrils often do when confronted by a pleasing aroma.

Whatever they were baking in there certainly smelled good.

He was tempted to tap on the window and ask if they could sell him a roll. He would take it home and have it with tea—or, better yet, eat it on the spot, as surely there was nothing better than a hot roll on a foggy London morning.

He bent over and peered through the glass. A number of people were busy at work with bread, but what surprised him was the manner of their costume. They were dressed in black gowns and had large yellow crosses suspended from their necks. Mark was no expert on baking or bakers, but he felt that this attire was not the standard for their profession. His gaze fell on one figure who was, in a most feminine manner, especially robust. The person's face was handsome, even beautiful, and she was engaged in kneading dough, her hands encased in white gloves. Another figure, of the male persuasion, approached her. He had red hair. They smiled at each other and spoke. The female figure then removed her right hand from the dough she was kneading, raised it up, and placed it on the head of the other.

Mark suddenly felt his mouth go dry and knew that, were the rolls produced by those hands the very last rolls in the world, he would not partake of one. He moved on and hid himself in the shadows.

A quarter of an hour later, a figure emerged from the doorway of the building and turned south-east on Archway Road.

Mark followed at a reasonable distance and observed as, a few hundred yards on, the fellow crossed the trafficless street and sat down at the bus stop. Mark approached. He stood and stared at the man for several moments.

"Hey, what's up, mate?" the fellow said.

"What were you doing?"

"What do you mean, mate?"

"I saw you come out of the bakery. What were you doing in there?"

"Um, baking, mate . . ."

Mark stared at him. The baker began to get nervous and stood up.

"Listen, mate, I don't want no trouble. I've got some good grass from Leeds. A couple of tokes mightn't do you bad."

Mark balled up his left hand into a fist, pulled it back and let it spring forward into the other's jaw. The fellow rocked on his feet for a moment and then fell backwards.

Mark looked him over. He was a clean-cut lad with no apparent tattoos or body piercings. This alone was enough to tell him that his suspicions were not unfounded.

Mark pulled out the dagger, kneeled down and thrust it to the other's throat.

"Look, mate, I'm just a breadhead. I ain't done nothin' wrong, I ain——"

The words drowned in a terrible lake of crimson.

Mark unzipped the man's backpack and looked through it. Inside was a notebook full of love letters, a ziplock bag with what seemed to be about an eighth of an ounce of marijuana, a pipe, and a dog-eared paperback titled, *The Book of the Two Principles*.

"I was right," Mark said to himself. "Those bakers are fucking Cathars!"

Friday

It was five o'clock. He hadn't been home all day. And what a day it had been. That morning, at 4:26, he had killed his fifth Cathar that week. Just as his blade had severed the carotid artery, a police whistle had sounded and he had spent the rest of the morning dashing about, running over housetops and trotting through sewers.

At 12:35 he had had a bowl of clam soup at a lunch counter near Waterloo Station and then he had idled away forty-five minutes in front of a florist shop before making his way to the Dandy Lad pub, where he had been sitting for the last three hours and twenty-six minutes drinking Three Tuns Golden Spicy Bitter, which he had heard from reliable sources had been the favorite beer of Algernon Blackwood.

He extracted his phone from his pocket and decided to check his e-mail. There was a single message in his inbox, from a Mr. George Tete, that looked promising. He opened it.

FROM THE DESK OF MR GEORGE TETE
THE BILL AND EXCHANGE MANAGER
BANK OF AFRICA (BOA)
OUAGADOUGOU-BURKINA FASO
WEST AFRICA BRANCH.
TEL: +226-66 23 93 30 +226-66 23 93 30

Dear Sir/Madam

I am contacting you based on trust and confidentiality that you will keep this as top secret.don't be scared or surprised, i am the Bill and Exchange Manager of BANK OF AFRICA and i have an opportunity to transfer sum of US($11.5.MILLION US DOLLARS) into your account.

I have the courage to look for a reliable and Honest Person who will be capable for this important business.Transaction,believing that you will never let me down either now or in Future.

The owner of this account is MR. ANDREAS SCHRANNER FROM MUNICH,GERMANY,.He died along side with his families in PLANE CRASH ON
31 JULY 2000. Since his death, the bank has made series of efforts to contact any of the relatives to claim this money but without success,And my investigation proved to me as well that his company does not know anything about this account.I want to transfer this money into a safe foreign account abroad but I don't know any foreigner,I know that this message will come to you as a surprise as we don't know ourselves before, but be sure that it is real and a Genuine business.

Hope that you will never let me down in this transaction, at the conclusion of this business, you will be giving 35% of the total amount, 65% will be for me.

I look forward to your earlier reply by email your full information's such as.

i)Your Full Name..
ii) Your Private Telephone Number........................
iii) Your Resident Address...................................
iv) A Scan Copy Of Your Passport if Any.......................

Thanks. Mr GEORGE TETE
BILL AND EXCHANGE MANAGER,
BANK OF AFRICA (BOA

He was just about to reply when his phone began to ring. It was Quentin S. Crisp. He answered and, after a few formalities, a rendezvous was arranged for an hour hence at the Three Salmons Pub.

"I guess I have time to knock off one more pint here before heading out."

And, on this matter, he was correct.

He arrived at his destination seven minutes before the designated time, went to the counter, got a pint of Old Brown Ale, a drink much admired by the great Arthur Machen, and then sat down at a table in the corner just beneath a portrait of James Hogg.

He took a sip of the glorious juice. It was like drinking a dark cloud blown in from the sea. After taking in about a third of his drink, he went and used the restroom. When he came out, he noticed Quentin just then walking in through the front door. The latter saw Mark Samuels and waved and then made a gesture indicating that he would join him in a moment. And, after purchasing a pint for himself, of Marston's Pedigree (the preferred drink of Yukio Mishima during his famous 1952 trip to London), he did, in fact, join him.

Quentin had longish hair and glasses. A green woolen scarf was wrapped around his neck. He was a typical product of North Devon—a vegetarian who had formed an early penchant for mermaid porn. But, just like everyone else from North Devon, he had no desire to live there and had found his home in London—that is if Bexleyheath could be called London, which would be akin to calling the man who scrapes bubblegum off the tracks along the District Line the Secretary of State for Transport.

Though his real passion was Brazilian wrestling, he made most of his money from ghostwriting for a British author by the name of Laiman Mangay.

Aside from his parish priest, Quentin was the only person in England Mark trusted.

"Hey," Mark said as Quentin sat down, setting his pint and an iPhone with a cracked screen on the table as he did so.

"Hello."

They each drank from their respective beers.

"So you heard about the killings?" Mark asked.

"Killings? No, I don't think so."

"Don't you read the newspapers?"

"Generally speaking, I only get my news from the *Living in the Future* webzine or whatever random links Brenpyon sends me."

"Brenpyon?"

"Yes, he is the one who is writing this story."

"I thought you were."

"No, mine is in the 'notes' app on my iPhone. I will read it to you if you like."

Mark said that, yes, he did like, and so Quentin picked up his iPhone, cleared his throat, and read aloud the following:

Nothing in time is eternal, but some things borrow eternity with such success that when they end we think the world itself has ended. Johnson, famously, thought London as large as life. The end of all things is kept from the consciousness of the Londoner as if by the Thames Barrier. "When I am rich," say the bells of Shoreditch. Though now such bells ring only in memory; in the present streets that voice is still the foot-passenger here may be so persuaded by London's commotion, still-going locomotion, prolific commerce and intermingling of enterprise and entropy that he is sharing in eternity, that even a doom dogging humanity as close as debt might be expected to dissipate here as if confronted by a reality with a greater credit rating than its own.

But what is the substance of this great credibility? In the central thoroughfares, though certain buildings stand firm against the centuries, the shuffling of money requires an effervescence of the new, a glass-and-concrete sparkle of inflationary bubbles that many sink beneath, and in this circulation of strangers all is change in the paper cup of a beggar on the pavement.

Is there nothing but this to London's borrowed eternity?

A hundred years and more ago, the Japanese novelist Natsume Sôseki, under an inky existential weight like a migraine of the soul, stopped at each intersection and unfolded his map, buffeted by those passing into shadow like this scene, so, too, will pass the young man in SkinnyJeans who stands here now, intent on his iPhone's GPS as he steps into traffic.

How the vastness of such turning seasons chills us! Yet the writer must hope to draw a thread between the disparate seasons, as Sôseki threaded those streets to him so hostile: as a spider holds together summer and autumn with its delicate web. The writer, in truth, is time's cartographer, and the most necessary thing for him to mark upon his map for future generations is where untainted drinking water might be found.

You are always the first point in the baseline from which you triangulate. Once you know the way here or there the crowd will be no longer just a crowd; you will discriminate which faces are old, which new, which buildings are ferned with tradition, which are the vigorous, illegitimate offspring of innovation. One thing separates from another, and in their separation their relation becomes clear. And presiding over these relations, unseen by most who tread the designated route of common sense, are the ghosts. Arthur Machen wrote of a fairy paradise visible to some at different times among the streets of Stoke Newington. On Peckham Rye, Blake saw a tree whose boughs were filled with angels. How much remains hidden? How much, though seen, untold? How much told among the obscure and unbelieved who, to the world of reputation and fame, are themselves as ghosts?

North of King's Cross, say the protagonists of Machen's Stoke Newington tale, we have left the known world behind us; if so, it is the unknown that will be our real starting point, but let us make our way by the known.

We find ourselves at London Bridge. A strange, fatalistic wind compels us and we sail down on the moving stairs to the Northern Line, watching the shine of the shoes, though they do not shine as in years past unless the haze of alcohol or pills makes it seem so, or the haze of melancholy itself; is it that in such a haze we see the Misery Line the shuffling tunnels that this black-inked section of the London underground acquired its unofficial name?

Pushed up like sedatives in the Tube of a hypodermic syringe as the plunger rises, we pass through Bank, Moorgate, Old Street, Angel, King's Cross St. Pancras, Euston (Bank branch), Camden Town (Bank branch), then swerving towards High Barnet we meet Kentish Town and Tufnell Park, and continue. If we have read the aforementioned tale by Machen, we might here remember the curious words of one of the characters concerning the elusive fairy garden: "You go in through a gateway, and . . . it [is] like finding yourself in another gateway." For, next, we come to Archway—surely, a gate. Yet beyond this gate is another, and greater—we have arrived at Highgate.

We seem to have attained a vantage from which we can look down upon London while still in London—look down upon geographically, but also as if historically, and even, perhaps, spiritually. There are places on the slowly rising hill from which at certain times of the day during certain times of year, we can see the street descend towards, and yet not meet, a strange suspension of an entire metropolis of rooftops among mist and cloud, as if that great, eternal city of the world, London, had only been a dream.

Ask and you might here, in lofty Highgate, in the eyrie of a top-floor flat, lives, drinks, writes and dreams another, such as Blake and Machen, who has seen beyond the seeming of London's mazy changes to the sure, unmoving flame whose shadows are our certainties: the sage of resignation, Mark Samuels, author, haunter of the bar, scryer of mysteries.

Let us now pass through the lofty gate and enter upon a point in time, as being enters the realm of becoming. Sunday, the 3rd of May, 2015. Samuels has visited, on the East Finchley Road, one of the capital's few remaining second-hand bookshops of note the copy of Evelyn Waugh's *A Little Order* in his hand, on its cover other hands, of that other author, a cigar between the fingers of the left, a pen in the right. These are a writer's totems; as there is a world apart from the world, so literature begets literature, and the writer invests in the paraphernalia of literary meditation. Samuels anticipates such meditation in his slow, measuring trudge along the Great North Road; he begins it, and the road becomes Archway Road, passing along the head of a bank, at the bottom of which runs a railway track on whose opposite side rises Highgate Wood.

Here let us pause, having entered time, and allow the tale to become past tense. It was one of those days in late spring or early summer when the sunshine has attained a golden mean between the imposition and the deprivation of heat; though such days are ephemeral they almost convince with their serenity that they are as everlasting as gold itself. A great, pacific friendliness of light was enlivened by now-and-then breezes just firm enough and delicate enough to tell you that a little sweat has moistened your brow. Samuels had drunk, before his excursion, sufficient to make the sunlight heady, his sensations as he glanced at the trackside Queen Ann's laced with sweet gusts of air as ale is with foam. The sun had brought out the bitter-fresh odor of the privet hedges, and now, as he walked along at the head of the railway bank, separated from him by a wire fence, where a little cool was made by trees and minor greenery anonymous as nursery rhyme, the odors of leaf and soil, in the gentle stew of sunlight, were as aromatic as a herb garden.

Samuels slowed and considered. We have long had means of recording sight and sound, but smell as yet has no medium in which it might be used to chronicle history. Perhaps if snails kept records, they would be primarily in smell, but for humans it is a sense whose tales are ghostlier even than the oral traditions of the unlettered. What story was this, told in scent? It was something long forgotten, but so deeply familiar it even reminded him of what words—dependent on the ones who speak or write—seldom did: that such a depth as this existed. Soil and sap. It was not just memory, he understood where he was on the pavement; that other world whose history was scent not word was as much alive as now is now. Still, what was it? There only came to him the thwack of ball hitting cricket bat, as if a riddle and its answer were contained in this sonic stereotype; and if the shell of this old chestnut could be cracked, its kernel would be fresh.

He continued. Between the spot where he had paused and the location of his flat there lay the Woodman, a pub with interior décor of humorless kitsch intended to be, perhaps, both tasteful and modern, but according to some observers, succeeding more nearly in creating the ambiance of a brothel. It also boasted, however, a pleasant beer garden with a good number of wooden tables, some of them sheltered in a flat-roofed wooden pavilion. It being Sunday, the weather fine, the breezes refreshing, and since he had received a cheque in the preceding week in payment for a tale, Samuels purchased a pint of Doom Bar here and took it outside to one of the tables in the roof-covered corner. He took his notebook from his shoulder bag, opened it in front of him, and wrote:

A chronicle of odors.

Laying down his pen, he picked up his pint and swigged, noticing as he did so a discarded *Metro* on the seat beside him. He swigged again, laid down his pint, picked up his pen once more and sat poised to harpoon with his nib any ideas that surfaced beneath his watchfulness. Where shadows had moved suggestively in those waters, now there was disappointing stillness.

If there's no inspiration, best not to write, he told himself, but his eye had returned to the discarded *Metro* and now he put down his pen as if finally and reached for the folded tabloid. He swigged again at his beer. Turning the inky pages, he became aware of a tarry fascination. What tobacco smoke did to the lungs, he felt, this was doing to his mind, but it was easy and gratifying and there was no immediate need to stop. Perhaps he could pick up ideas here, anyway, for topical window-dressing to be used, as the need arose, in future stories. Not that he cared about these particular topics. "A ban on legal highs" mentioned in the Queen's Speech, though to ban what is legal is a contradiction in terms; a Danish radio presenter—vegetarian?—battered a rabbit to death on air to highlight the hypocrisy of not being vegetarian, but did anyone eat the rabbit he had killed in order to highlight the hypocrisy of killing a rabbit as a protest against killing animals? Gwen Stefani took a 'brelfie'—a breastfeeding selfie—to tackle the stigma of breastfeeding, but there was a backlash—breastlash?—since "putting new mums under 'bressure' benefits no one," said Siobhan Freegard.

Samuels tossed the tabloid back on the seat where he had found it, not wishing to read more and now more than ever trapped in the concatenation of mere thought of which writer's block is made. He glanced around at the friends (to each other) and couples drinking at the nearby tables, and at the strangers, dressed for summer, passing the garden on the pavement beyond. The tabloid was a scrabble of competing greeds and grievances, glued together with unspoken lies. One might have imagined it revealed the death struggle of the human soul—two people rolling around at a cliff edge with their hands at each other's throats—but that struggle was in no way apparent in his immediate environment, so that the paper was an enigma, like the Serpent in Eden.

From nowhere, then, breaking the small, irrefutable chain of the inevitable, there came a thought as vast and simple as day: I would like to write a tale of wonder.

It was not a new thought, except inasmuch as it was always new, always waiting.

What was it that distracted him from this end? What delayed him?

He rolled his pen upon the tabletop with his fingertips as he pondered this question. There only formed in his mind the phrase "a fallen world," but he could not make an answer of this and groped, instead, in his pocket, for his e-cigarette.

As he leaned into himself to retrieve his vape stick, the world that had occupied his thoughts was eclipsed by the approach of a human figure. Like a comet's tail of blue smoke, a dragon coiled around his arm, its head towards his hand as if in plummeting descent.

Samuels raised his head.

"I haven't seen you for a while," said the newcomer.

"Oh, hello Dane," said Samuels, moving up to make room.

"Where have you been?"

"Around. How about you?"

"The same. Looking for a mead hall."

"Mead hall? Oh. I think we've all become wanderers since they closed the Colchester Arms. I bump into old regulars, like you, now and then, by chance, but no one seems to settle on one place anymore, as if they've lost their orbit."

Quentin put down his iPhone, picked up his pint, and took a 'swig'.

"Um, yeah," Mark said, "anyhow—about the killings . . ."

"Yes?"

"I've killed five people this week."

"I see," Quentin replied. He lifted his ale to his lips and took a sip, then set it back down on its coaster. "And how did this come about?"

In rather colorful language, which is to say blending cadences of Oliver

Onions with pleasant overtones of Charles Dickens and a few quirky asides *à la* Bloy, Mark described what had happened the night before.

"So, if I understand you correctly," Quentin said, "you killed these people because you suspected that they were Cathars?"

"It wasn't a suspicion."

"They were Cathars and you killed them?"

"That's right. Do you think I did the wrong thing?"

"I wouldn't go so far as to say that. As you know, I could scarcely be called a fan of Catharism, being myself more inclined to the teachings of Lao Tzu. I am just not sure that, um, killing these chaps can forward your stylistic mission unless you can somehow integrate it."

"Integrate it?"

"Yes, it seems to me that if you could make this an integral part of your thought process, it might benefit your future work. If a person is deaf, they can't hear even Manowar. If a person is blind, they couldn't even see Kate Beckinsale if she was stripped naked before them. That is why in some situations sign language is necessary, while in others experiments in direct perception are required. In 1885 Vincent van Gogh painted *The Potato Eaters*. In 1637 Dutch tulip prices collapsed. Ovid was exiled by Augustus. Hokoji Temple at Nara took twenty years to complete. Spinning through space, don't forget to take stock of dry land. When committing murder, it is considered prudent to leave no traces. I would also suggest studying the *Chin Yen Ching* and the *Wan Pi Kau ch'iu Hsien Sheng Fa*."

Mark swallowed down the last of his beer. Quentin realized that he was lagging behind somewhat, so finished his off and then rose from his seat to get another round. He returned soon with a pair of pints.

Quentin's iPhone was making a beeping, bubbling sound. He picked it up and looked at it.

"J-bon is calling me on Skype."

"J-bon?"

"Justin Isis."

Mark stood up and went around to the other side of the table so he could see the phone.

Quentin pressed the answer button and a lean, handsome face appeared behind the crack on the screen. Next to him was a Japanese woman with an easy-going appearance.

"Hey, me and Mika are sitting here in my apartment with some Ozeki OneCups."

"Markitty and I are at the Three Salmons Pub."

"Markitty?" Mark asked.

"Yes, that's your kawaii sobriquet," Q-bon replied.

Markitty and Q-bon both looked at the iPhone. J-bon was speaking.

"Did massive DMT last night. Went far off the grid. It was eternity outside time and space and I broke through far far more than before, like a billion times. Earlier experience was more like some kind of veil or outer realm with those nymphs or spirits. This was off in the hypersphere where I also met the goddess. Unbelievably terrifying, though in a non-Euclidean sense—time as solid physical dimension."[1]

"Which goddess was it?" Q-bon asked.

"Isis."

---

1. Justin here again. . . . If you're enjoying this book, please consider picking up *Pleasant Tales II*, written by me and forthcoming from Snuggly Books. There is one story I didn't have enough space to include and that I will summarize here: Alan Ladd, the American actor who found success in the 1940s and early 1950s with Westerns such as *Shane* (1953) and film noirs where he was often paired with Veronica Lake, is preparing the lethal combination of alcohol and tranquillizers that will lead to his death on January 29th, 1964, when he is visited by a time traveling dolphin named Ecco, who explains that he was moved enough by Ladd's performance in *Boy on a Dolphin*, the 1957 romantic film set in Greece and shot in DeLuxe Color and CinemaScope and featuring also the English-language debut of Sophia Loren, that he petitioned the Earth Coincidence Control Office (E.C.C.O) with the intention of reconciling Ladd to his true position in the universal order before allowing him to face his inevitable end. Ecco has brought Alan Ladd seventeen tabs of AL-LAD—also known as 6-allyl-6-nor-LSD, an analogue of lysergic acid diethylamide synthesized from LSD using allyl bromide as a reactant—as well as a variety of synthetic cannibanoids and bath salts. Alan Walbridge Ladd (September 3, 1913 – January 29, 1964), whose other notable credits include *Two Years Before the Mast* (1946), *Whispering Smith* (1949) and *The Great Gatsby* (1949), is intrigued by the dolphin's timeless smooth skin not ageing like all boys must. His slick renown diminished in the late 1950s, though he continued to appear in popular films until his accidental death due to a lethal combination of alcohol, a barbiturate, and two tranquillizers. Ecco blasts the seventeen tabs from his blowhole and onto the popular American actor's tongue. AL-LAD in, Alan Ladd is led like a lad insane to an Aladdin's cave of hyperbolic time

"I see."

"What was she like?" Mark asked.

"It was like meeting someone face to face after only previously talking to them online. I tried to trade with the joker/spirit/god things by giving them letters from the alphabet I'm working on. I'm limiting the current sequence to just ten letters/compounds, three verbs and two pronouns. It's more like a spell or something anyway."

"I would go easy on the DMT," Mark said. "My friend was a missionary in Brazil and started doing a lot of hallucinogens and I think it affected him sort of permanently."

"Yeah?"

"Yes, he still considers Jesus to be his lord and savior, but is also part of an ayahuasca cult."

"I wish I were an ayahuasca cult," Q-bon said.

---

solids (known to humans as 'coincidences') that manifest acausal connecting principles in the manner of Leibniz's monads. Now equipped with an experiential understanding of panpsychic Idealism, Alan Ladd returns to the scene of his death, barbiturate synergy slow spasm sound-tracked by Ecco singing in ultrasound over *Chuck Person's Eccojams Vol. 1* by Daniel Lopatin a.k.a. Oneohtrix Point Never. Alan Ladd riding the sexual compassion flying dolphin hearing his death in an echo. The dolphin cresting the waters of time Alan Ladd's penis nervous smile as Shane. Alan Ladd bath salts taking the curving dolphin penis in his mouth and accepting the eucharistic wellness before dying free from fear of universal lovelessness, stepping back into his death as into an old and well-fitting suit, synthetic cannibanoids invading time incautious and entire. Golden riding boy statue in curved pallid Alan Ladd wounded nervous shadow out of time and unloved beneath this wandering gun.

> You say, "he's only a statue, and what can a statue achieve?"
> And yet, while I'm gazing at you,
> My heart tells my head to believe.
>
> If the boy whom the gods have enchanted
> Should arise from the sea,
> And the wish of my heart could be granted,
> I would wish that you loved only me.

J-bon nodded his head. "In the non-Euclidean dimension you are."

"Hey, the battery on my iPhone is on ten percent. I should say good-bye now."

"Okay, cool," J-bon said, and then turned to the Japanese woman who was saying something to him in a low voice.

"Hey, Mika wants to say something to Markitty."

"Hi Mika!" Markitty said.

The woman smiled and then, obviously nervous, spoke:

"I. Can be. On your. Album cover?"

After the Skype conversation, Mark and Quentin sat across from each other drinking their beers. They both felt empty. Quentin was vaguely imagining what it would be like to live in Krylatyy. Mark was recalling the look on his first victim's face as he had seen the dagger. He had looked like a bad actor playing Hamlet.

Quentin lifted his glass high and let the beer spill down his throat. A moment later, empty, it clunked down on the table.

"I should be heading back to Bexleyheath," he said.

"And I to Highgate."

They both rose from their seats and strolled past the loo, on the door of which was written 'Gentlemen'—both lads thinking at that very instant that if everyone who went in there were really gentle, the world would be a much finer place.

They stepped outside. The sidewalk was bustling with people. Quentin flung the left side of his scarf over his shoulder so that his chin became partially concealed. Without speaking, they walked to Angel tube station and descended the stairs. Each man needed to go in the opposite direction of the other.

"Goodbye," Mark said.

"Bye," Quentin answered.

Thirty-two minutes later Mark was standing before Kiplings Restaurant and Bar, on Hill Street.

He looked in his mailbox. There was an envelope, addressed to him in a bold, rolling script. He opened it, and found within the following letter:

Dear Mr. Samuels,

Your incapability to pay me, with convenience to yourself, the month's rent which is due from you, is, I assure you, sufficient apology for any little disappointment which the delay may occasion to me. I am convinced of your wish to be punctual, and, therefore, cheerfully assent to your request. Let the month's rent stand over as you desire, and give yourself no uneasiness on the subject. I shall not ask you for it until after the current month has ceased and the next begun, long ere which, I trust, the anxieties of which you complain will have vanished.

I am, sir,

Your obedient servant,

Eumolpus Patric

Lotus Flowers, Lotus Leaves

Cassidy took one last hit off the roach and then dropped it in the ashtray.

He remembered his past life when he had been João III, King of Portugal, and realized that he should try his hardest to become a better spirit and increase his capacity for love and charity.

"If I want to see my divine reflection," he thought, "I need to make sure not to be thwarted on the path."

He was 5'8", 135 pounds, and had blond hair that was already beginning to thin even though he was only twenty-three years old. His father, a descendant of Irish immigrants, had once told him that he should become a truck driver and he sometimes thought that his father might have been right.

"Fuck," Evan said.

Evan was a big guy with dark brown hair and a scrimpy beard. He was wearing a black T-shirt with nothing written on it and a pair of black jeans.

"I wish I had a Rice Crispie treat," Cindy said.

"Don't we all."

"My mom makes them with two parts Rice Crispies to one part Fruity Peb——"

"Fruity Pebbles are too sweet," Evan said.

"Whatever."

Evan looked at Cindy and blinked. She was a tomboy and, in fact, most people would not have even realized that she was a girl, but he had been in love with her for some time now. He was worried, however, that if he told her how he felt, she would say that he wasn't her type. He was also pretty sure that if he ever managed to get together with her, the other guys would make fun of him, though that aspect didn't bother him very much since his sister had once told him that he had an IFES personality type.

"Sure, she looks exactly like a boy," Evan thought, "but I bet she's more woman than most guys could handle."

Trevor was shaking his head.

"You guys do realize, don't you, that all that stuff you're talking about is total genetically modified crap? Rice Crispie treats? Fuck that shit. Give me a Clif Bar at least."

"I'd rather have a Clif Bar too," Cassidy said, "but right now would take anything."

Trevor frowned.

He had short dreadlocks and a small amount of facial hair. He had been born in New Jersey but, obsessed with cowboys, had run away at the age of sixteen to go work on a ranch in Wyoming. After five years of ranching, however, he had realized that he just didn't fit in and had hitchhiked to California where he was presently employed as a full-time puzzle assembler.

The night before, he had dreamt that he was in Sweden. He was walking through a forest barefoot and he came to a pool of water. It wasn't water, however, but sweat. He was then sitting on a pier. A man came up to him. He had red hair and introduced himself as Sven and said that he was a psychic. He told Trevor that he, Trevor, needed to acquire a talisman to protect himself from pterodactyls.

"Don't you have anything at all to eat in your fridge?" Trevor asked Cassidy.

"No, I don't."

"I bet I can find something," Cindy said.

She got up, went to the kitchen and opened the refrigerator door.

`There was nothing inside but a half-full jar of Lily of the Desert aloe vera juice, some yeast, and a jar of organic brown mustard. She went back to the living room and told everyone that the only things in Cassidy's fridge were a half-full jar of Lily of the Desert aloe vera juice, some yeast, and a jar of organic brown mustard.

"Let's order a pizza," Trevor suggested.

"Mark & Johnny's rocks," Cassidy said.

"BEST PIZZA IN THE FUCKING WORLD."

"Yeah," Trevor said, "they're, like, a national treasure."

"Their crust has the crunch."

"They have really good pest——" Cindy was starting to say.

"Their pesto pizza is primo," Evan cut in.

"They use locally sustainable ingredients," Trevor said.

Cassidy picked up his iPhone, called the pizzeria and ordered a large pesto pizza and was told it would be delivered in about thirty or thirty-five minutes.

Everyone smiled and nodded their heads in anticipation of the pizza.

"Might as well smoke another one while waiting," Evan said, taking a bag of weed out of his jeans pocket.

"I dunno," Trevor said, "I'm pretty stoned. Need to eat something first."

"You'll be eating, like, by the time the joint's done. Just be cool."

While Evan was rolling a large joint Cassidy docked his iPhone on the stereo and clicked in to his 'Eyeliner & Cloves' playlist. A song by Racey called 'Boy, Oh Boy' began to play.

Trevor tapped the fingers of his right hand on his right knee as if he were playing a tiny drum.

Evan lit the joint, took a puff, and handed it to Cindy, looking directly in her eyes as he did so.

"Do you guys believe in past lives?" Cassidy asked.

Evan nodded his head.

"I do," he said. "The other day I was watching a YouTube video about sexy cam funny laugh pranks and suddenly remembered when I was a fisherman in the year 1287. I had a wife and two children. It was raining all the time and it was really hard to keep dry. We weren't wearing real clothing, but these, like, thick skins. There was some sort of dark force from the spirit realm that kept trying to hurt me. It was, like, a level 4 difficulty and I realized that I was going to have to reincarnate to fulfill my mission in density."

"That's pretty cool," Cassidy said.

"Sometimes when I smoke weed," Trevor said, exhaling a cloud of smoke, "I go into a deep alpha state. This little voice in my head tells me to close my eyes. So I close them and start to see weird visuals, like all these geometric sine waves and cosine waves weaving in and out of each other. A few weeks ago this happened and I suddenly realized I was in the middle of a redwood tree. My spirit vision stretched out into infinity and the connection with my pineal gland kept expanding until my life and memories never existed."

"Cannabis can definitely be helpful in bringing you into your own body," Cassidy said.

Evan had a sad, far-away look in his eyes.

"Sometimes I feel like I'm living in a book," he said. "I'm living in a book, but, like, the chapters are out of order."

"I completely feel you man," Trevor said. "It's called derealization."

"It's like my brain and body are two different things," Evan continued. "I look at myself in the mirror and just see ancient Nordic runes and start to feel that everything around me is fake. Or maybe we're all just random sparks on this condensed complex carbon molecules ball that we call our planet. We're workers and our goal is to just experience, and our experiences are transferred into the Cloud, which is the source, the infinite semantic energy that contains all of our futures, and our connection to the very first organism."

Everyone sat silent for a moment, deeply affected by Evan's words

"Hey, guys?" Cindy said presently.

"Yeah, what?"

"Didn't we, like, um, order that——"

"We ordered that pie an hour ago!" Evan cut in.

Cassidy said he would call the pizzeria, and he did.

"Hey, this is Cassidy Locrasto-Friedman at 3278 D Street," he said. "I ordered a pesto pie like an hour ago and it still hasn't got here."

"Yeah? Juan left with it forty minutes ago. He should have got there and back by now."

"He never came."

The man at the pizzeria sounded annoyed. He said he would track Juan down and call Cassidy back. Cassidy wondered if they often had problems with Juan.

He pressed the end call button on his iPhone.

"So?" Evan asked.

"The pizza was sent out for delivery forty minutes ago."

"Something must have gone awry," Trevor said.

"Fuck it, we can't wait around here forever while our blood sugar is plummeting. Let's just go get some Chinese food."

"I AM A CHINESE FOOD LOVER!"

"Luweeh's Kitchen?"

"Yeah, that's the shit. Their pea sprouts rock."

"Wor wonton soup."

"We can take my car," Evan said. "It's more spacious than Cassidy's."

Everyone agreed. They got up, put on their jackets and headed out the door.

It was a gloomy night in October. It had rained earlier and the sidewalks were wet. Leafless trees stood gray and ominous against the sky.

Everyone was about to pile into Evan's SUV, when Cindy noticed that one of the tires was flat.

"More than one," Trevor said. "They're all flat."

Evan was very angry.

"Someone's a major dickhead," he said.

"Let's just take my car," Cassidy said.

Cassidy drove a subcompact hatchback with an 'I Used to be Cool' bumper sticker. He took out his keys and walked to the driver's-side door. Looking down, he perceived that the front tire was flat. He walked around the car and saw that, just like Evan's SUV, all four of the tires of his vehicle were also, in fact, flat.

"Looks like someone slashed my tires too," he said. "It's probably a neighbor."

"Your neighbors slash your tires?"

"I dunno. There's some old man living next door who is always looking over the wall. He was complaining about my dog barking. It could have been him."

"You have a dog?"

"No."

Everyone went back inside, took off their jackets and sat down. No one said anything at first. Trevor had a scared look on his face and Evan looked depressed.

A heavy mood had set in. Cassidy thought about turning on some music, going back to his 'Eyeliner & Cloves' playlist, but decided not to. He felt confused and didn't think music would help—and the only music that might have fit the situation anyhow would have been Sebastián Aguilera de Heredia's 'Tiento de Falsas de Quarto Tono', but he didn't have that on his iPhone.

Cindy went and got glasses of water for everyone.

"We have to keep hydrated," she said.

"I think we should call the police," Trevor said.

"Fuck the police," Evan said. "If they showed up they'd probably end up arresting us. Then once they have us in their car they'll sodomize us and kill us."

"The tire situation is peculiar," Cindy said.

"Me and my friend Joe were once hanging out by the American River," Cassidy said. "We parked his van and got out and went down to the river and started drinking a bottle of chilled white wine. We were talking about how atoms work and how our bodies work with chemical and electrical impulses and how random evolutionary natural selection gives us humans and chimpanzees. Only a few rearranged atoms separate the two, and yet from those we get art, language and mathematics. Humans have anxiety that brings us suffering and holds us back from progressing emotionally. Many people never share their experiences and achievements, because the reward is intrinsic and not dependent on others approving and validating those experiences and achievements."

"But, um, something happened to the van?" Trevor asked.

"No, the van was fine." ·

Evan was nodding his head and wondering what to say when there was a knock on the door.

"I bet it's the piz———"

"It's gotta be the pizza," Evan said, finally finding the words he had been searching for.

"Well, the delivery guy's not getting a tip, that's for sure."

"It's probably cold."

"Who gives a fuck," Evan said, and laughed.

Cassidy opened the door. But it wasn't the pizza delivery guy, it was Dimitri.

"Hey," Dimitri said.

"Hey," Cassidy replied. He stood at the door hesitatingly looking at Dimitri. He thought about making some excuse so he wouldn't have to let Dimitri in, but couldn't think of one, so ended up just saying, "Come on in."

Dimitri walked in and nodded his head.

He was 5'6", 148 lbs, with brown hair and glasses. He looked like he hadn't shaved or taken a shower for a few days, but he always looked like that.

Everyone seemed uncomfortable. No one really liked Dimitri. He was one of those characters that have a difficult time making real friends and who are generally avoided by their peers.

"So, looks like everyone's here HAVING A GOOD TIME," he said. "No one ever calls me, and I was in the 'hood, so figured I'd just drop by. Didn't realize you guys were having a PARTY."

"We're not," Trevor said.

"Nope," Evan agreed.

"We thought you were the pizza delivery guy," Cindy said.

"You ordered a pizza?"

"Yeah, over an hour ago."

"If you ordered it over an hour ago, and it's not here yet, it's never going to come. Those pizza guys are mostly drug addicts. He probably traded your pizza to someone for some crack and is smoking it right now."

"Maybe," Cassidy said.

"Whatever *you're* smoking, smells damned good," Dmitri said.

"Yeah."

"Now you guys got the munchies I bet?"

"No, we're just hungry," Cindy said.

"We were going to go to Luweeh's Kitchen, but someone slashed all the tires on my car and Evan's too."

"Someone slashed your tires?" Dimitri said.

"Yeah."

"Was probably the pizza guy. I bet last time you ordered a pie you gave him a shitty tip and this time he just said 'Fuck it' and bladed your tires."

"We need food," Trevor said.

Dimitri let out a high pitched laugh.

"You guys should just come over to my place," he said. "I've got all sorts of food and snacks there. I went shopping today at Whole Foods and spent a ton of money."

"I dunno."

"I've got peppermint bark, peanut butter, Nutella, potato chips, corn chips," Dimitri said. "I also have some of that kung pao tofu, and a bunch of turkey picadillo, apricot chicken tangine, and about a half-gallon of Italian white bean soup. And I've got beverages too—a bunch of cans of coconut water and an unopened bottle of carrot-tangerine juice."

Everyone looked at each other questioningly. No one really trusted Dimitri but they were all hungry and thought that maybe he was telling the truth.

"You know," Evan said, "it's not like we don't trust you, but I've been dicked around so many times in my life that I tend to proceed with caution. What if we all show up there and, like, we find out you were bullshitting us? Not only that, but both Cassidy's vehicle and my own are incapacitated, and don't you, like, um, drive a moped?"

"Yes, I DO drive a moped. But I can carry someone on the back. I live over on 19th and J—that's only twenty blocks away. I can just ferry you guys over one at a time. No problemo."

There was a moment of silence and then Trevor spoke:

"I don't know about the rest of you guys, but I think Dimitri's offer sounds awesome. I'm happy to go over there and confirm things though."

Dimitri seemed excited.

"So you guys up for it then?" he said. "You ready to hang out at MY house and PARTY DOWN?"

Everyone agreed that it seemed like the best option and Dimitri said he would shuttle Trevor back to his house and then return for the next person.

Everyone went to the door and watched as Dimitri and Trevor got on the former's moped and left the scene. The sound of the moped could be heard as it sped away up the street

"I hope Trevor is okay," Cassidy said, closing the door. "Dimitri is pretty weird."

"I think he's okay," Evan said. "I mean, yeah, he sort of gives me the creeps too, but I think his heart is in the right place. He probably suffers from shyness and makes up for it by being rude and pushy."

"Yeah," Cindy started saying, "just because he has poor social skills doesn't mean——"

"Just because he has poor social skills, it doesn't mean he's innately evil," Evan cut in.

A few minutes later Cassidy's iPhone rang. It was Trevor.

"Over here at Dimitri's," he said. "It turns out he wasn't bullshitting at all. Understating if anything. His fridge is packed. There's a huge bag of walnuts too. He's also got a couple six-packs of craft beer."

"So, game on," Cassidy said.

"Cool," Trevor said. "I'll set up some peanut butter Nutella nachos while waiting for you guys."

Cassidy relayed the information to Cindy and Evan.

"Dimitri always seemed like an asshole to me," Evan said, "but he's being pretty cool tonight."

"I think we all need to allow others the option of personal growth," Cassidy said. "Sometimes seeing others as they really are, requires us to make a shift of view. If we reject all the negativity we feel around us we can become better people and make other people better also."

"Isn't being down on negativity pretty negative itself?" Evan said. "Remember the wise words of Matthew: Give not that which is holy unto the dogs, neither cast ye your pearls before swine, lest they trample them under their feet, and turn again and rend you."

"You're Christian?"

"Fuck no. I'm a Taoist."

Both Cassidy and Cindy looked at Evan with skepticism.

"The tao is the nameless source of everything," Evan said. "Life is the greatest teacher. Wisdom is succumbing to freedom. If you're not appreciated by your own self, don't expect others to appreciate you. I try to be a good friend to myself and it's up to others to do the same. A good competitor rejoices in defeat the same as victory."

Just then there was a quick rap on the door and it swung open.

It was Dimitri.

"Who's next?" he asked.

"Um, why don't you, um, take Cassidy," Evan said.

Cassidy looked at Cindy. She was twisting her lips, making an unpleasant expression.

"No, it's okay," Cassidy said. "Why doesn't Cindy go next."

"Right, ladies first and all that," Evan said, looking at Cindy.

"Don't be sexist, Evan. Why don't you——"

"Okay, yeah, fuck it, if everyone's so damned indecisive I'll go and see you guys in a few mins."

Evan and Dimitri left.

Cassidy and Cindy sat there.

"I'm glad Dmitri took Evan instead of you," Cindy said.

"Yeah, well, this is my place, so I should be the last to leave I guess."

"Still . . ."

"You don't like Evan?"

"Well, I think he's got a crush on me. Have you noticed how he's always looking at me?"

"Um, not really. But I'm usually pretty cerebral, so I often don't notice the physical trappings around me. But it's sort of weird if Evan likes you and never says anything."

"I dunno."

"It's probably from a fear of rejection."

"Yeah, a judicious fear."

"So, you'd reject him?"

"Well, he's just not my type."

"What is your type?"

"Hmm," Cindy said and looked thoughtful for a moment. "You know, it's not that visual attraction is the most important thing, but it is relevant."

"You don't think Evan is visually attractive?"

"No, I don't. For one thing, he has a beard, which, for me, is a giant germy turn-off. He also, um, always cuts me off when I speak, and I don't like that. If I ever found a man, and I doubt I will—but if I ever did, I would want to be with someone who is physically and spiritually balanced. A man who is both unjudgmental and who doesn't let himself be controlled by his body's agenda. Someone who is willing to challenge the status quo and who isn't afraid of the abyss. I like guys who ride motorcycles, but that isn't really important. The most important thing for a woman—I mean for me at least—is to have a sense of comradeship. I want an anchor, not a boat floating adrift."

"That's cool," Cassidy said.

There was a moment of silence and then Cindy spoke:

"I really liked what you said earlier."

"What, you mean about when I was down by the river with my friend Joe?"

"No, about us rejecting negativity so we can become better people and make others better too."

"I sometimes think the purpose of life is to become a better person, and one can't become a better person without helping others succeed, right?"

"Are you a white knight?"

Cassidy laughed. "No," he said. "I'm just on a path, like everyone is. Infinity doesn't have an end. Sometimes we ebb and sometimes we flow—both part of the whole and the whole at the same instant. We———"

At that moment the front door sprang open and Dimitri walked in. He looked tired.

"You okay?" Cindy asked.

"All this going back and forth, man . . ."

"Yeah, well, we appreciate it."

Dimitri asked Cindy if she was ready to go and she said that she was.

Cindy looked at Cassidy and smiled.

"Well, bye," she said.

"See you soon."

"Yeah."

She looked directly in his eyes for less than a second, then turned and left.

"Be back in a flash," Dimitri said and gave an uneasy laugh.

Cassidy sat alone on the couch. He didn't feel like being alone and would be glad to be over at Dimitri's with everyone else. He started thinking about what Cindy had said. He understood why she was not attracted to Evan. If he, Cassidy, had been a woman, he too would not have been attracted to him.

He had never thought about her as a potential girlfriend, but he now wondered if such a thing were possible. He had, for some time now, been tired of being single. He wanted to get married and have a family. He thought he would make a good husband and father.

"You might be able to get her," the voice inside him said. "She feels safe with you."

"Evan is a lot bigger and stronger than I am," Cassidy replied.

"Physical strength isn't the only thing that makes a woman feel safe. But if you really want to win her heart, you have to give her a nickname."

"A nickname? Wouldn't that just piss her off?"

"No, it would make her feel cared for. It would make a special connection between you and her."

"What sort of nickname would you suggest?"

"Cinnamon or Kat-Kat."

"Kat-Kat seems sort of nice."

"It's a winner."

"So, um, do you think Cindy—do you think Kat-Kat would actually have sex with me?"

"She hasn't rejected you, so this means that she is definitely poised to consider it. If you're emotionally open with her, she will likely be physically open with you. You can't swim without getting wet. Intimacy requires vulnerability. She, too, is a primate and will wish to reproduce with the most worthy mate."

Cassidy suddenly realized that he was no longer hungry. He felt strangely clear and refreshed, as if he had just bathed in a jungle pool. It seemed as if the thin, pink bubble that had been surrounding him had broken.

The front door opened.

It was Dimitri. His features were drawn out. He looked like he had aged a great deal.

"Ready to go?" he asked.

"Yeah."

Cassidy got up from the couch, put on his jacket, and walked outside with Dimitri.

He then locked the door behind him.

The Doorman

Though Carla's job was an assistant store manager at the Family Dollar Store, the Lord God had made it so that her real ambition was to be a novelist. The fifty-eight pages she had written of her work in progress, *The Doorman*, had not come easy—in fact it had been a terrifying experience—but through hard work and prayer, she had come that far.

"I'm so proud of you," her husband, Wyatt, said one night at dinner.

Hearing Wyatt say this filled Carla with an overwhelming sense of joy.

"I have only been able to travel this far due to the help of Our Lord God Jesus Christ," she replied modestly.

"That's true," Wyatt observed, "but not all who are called answer. You were called and you answered. That counts for a lot."

"Thanks, Wyatt," Carla said and put a bite of chicken noodle casserole in her mouth.

"You need to start looking for a publisher."

"But, honey, the book isn't done yet."

Wyatt picked up a yeast roll and started buttering it.

"I've heard," he said, "that writers often look for the publisher *before* the book is done."

Carla was so happy that Wyatt was in her life and that evening, after he had fallen asleep, she prayed fervently over him, thanking the Lord that she had this man to help shelter her from the storms of life, this man who was both generous with touch and words of affirmation.

The next day, at work, while she was neatening up some bars of Venezia Soapworks lemon verbena moisturizing soap, she began to ponder what Wyatt had said the night before.

Brett Murray, the store manager, walked up near her.

"Looks great," he said, motioning towards the soap shelf with his right hand.

"Thanks, Brett," Carla said.

"A little preoccupied about something, Carla?"

"Well, Brett—I've just been wondering how I can receive the spirit of wisdom."

"Wisdom?"

"The book I'm writing—*The Doorman*—just wondering how I can get it published."

"Well, I'm just a store manager of a Family Dollar Store, Carla, so that is out of my purview. If you want to know how to do something, ask someone who has done it before."

And so it was that God, in His loving mercy, shone a light in the darkness for Carla, and Carla, grateful to Brett, who had been the instrument of the Lord, offered grace and prayed for him.

"Yes," she thought, "Brett is right. If I want to publish my book, I need to ask advice from someone who has done it before—a successful writer."

Unfortunately, she didn't know any successful writers, and in this felt strongly her own vulnerability. She prayed hard, day after day, and fasted, and on the seventh day, the Lord God had mercy on her, and helped her to embrace His design.

That day the soles of her feet had felt rather dry, like they needed extra moisture and she knew, in her heart, that washing them with Venezia Soapworks lemon verbena moisturizing soap would not be enough, and so, after work, she had stopped at Peace of Mind Oils to get some essential lavender oil. After purchasing the oil, as she was walking back to her car, she noticed that a few shops down was a store called Brian's Books. Carla, putting her trust in God and thereby overcoming doubts and fears, walked in.

The store was full of books—books that had been published—and Carla knew that she too would, through the power of Christ, become a fruitful vine.

A lean young man with red hair sat behind a desk, reading.

"Excuse me," Carla said.

"Yeah?"

"Are you Brian?"

"No, Brian's not here right now. I'm Paul."

"A beautiful name."

"Thanks."

"My name is Carla Jo Arduini."

"Nice. Looking for something?"

"In a sense . . . yes. Maybe you can help me?"

"Sure."

"I would like to know . . ."

"Know?"

". . . the name of a . . ."

"A book?"

"No, a . . ."

"An author?"

Carla smiled, realizing that God had not only set the stage, but had also written the script.

"Yes," she said, "I would like to know the name of an author—a famous author."

"Famous?"

"Uh-huh. What's that book you're reading?"

"It's a book by, um, Laird Barron."

"Is he famous?"

"Well, yeah, I guess so—in the genre."

"The . . . genre?"

"Yeah, well, you probably wouldn't like it."

But, God had guided her and she, thrilled to be of service to him, purchased a copy of the book in question.

"Thank you, Dear Lord," she said, with tears in her eyes, as she drove home. "Thank you for helping me overcome my challenges, and for allowing me to move at the sound of Your voice!"

When she told Wyatt what had happened, he nodded his head knowingly. "The Lord takes care of those He created," he said. "Don't ever imagine that you're going to be abandoned, Carla, by Him or me. Remember, God gives good gifts to those He loves."

That night, after touch, Carla picked up the book she had purchased and stared at the cover.

"Laird Barron needs to read *The Doorman*," her spirit said within her.

She opened the book and began reading. After reading four pages, she realized that, though written with an undeniable prowess, it most certainly was not in line with Scripture.

"Perhaps," she said to herself, "God is offering me an opportunity to go deeper into Him. Perhaps there is a Holy Purpose in the words I am reading."

Finding Laird Barron on Twitter was much easier than she had thought it would be—so easy, in fact, that, when she did, she couldn't help but murmur, "God has led me to this day."

She had logged into her account, @drowningingod, which she hadn't used in six months, and immediately accorded Jesus a hashtag:

> I'm smiling thinking of
> someone. #Jesus

She went to Laird Barron's account and clicked on the 'Follow' tab.

She scrolled through his tweets. Most of them were links to book reviews or him saying things that she didn't understand. But just then, as she was looking, a mysterious and bewildering thing happened. A new tweet appeared on the screen:

> Doing reading at
> Fayetteville Public
> Library tomorrow at
> 1:30. Please come!

She blinked, shook her head, and looked again. The tweet was still there!

Fayetteville? It was only one hundred and ninety-two miles away!

Tears came into her eyes when she realized that God had guided her there, at that blessed time, to see that special tweet!

It was clear that the Lord God had listened to her prayers and that the fellowship of the Holy Spirit was with her. He had, indeed, chosen her as His cherished treasure.

The next day was a Saturday. During breakfast, she told Wyatt that she would not be attending Bible Study with him because she was going to Fayetteville.

"Fayetteville?" Wyatt said. "That's a long way away. May I ask the reason for the journey?"

"It's my novel, *The Doorman*. Today is the day when my heart shall be made to rest easier."

And she told Wyatt about Laird Barron's miraculous tweet from the night before.

"You have to go to Fayetteville, Carla," he said. "God wants you to go to Fayetteville. You have to go."

"I know I do, Wyatt."

After cleaning up the breakfast things and taking a long, hot shower, she printed out the full fifty-eight pages of *The Doorman* and secured it with a heavy-duty binder clip. She then packed a bag of spiced nuts and a few Cokes and, after giving Wyatt touch, departed on her journey.

As has been indicated, the journey from Rose Bud to Fayetteville was not a short one, but Carla was determined not to lose the chance that God had put in her way.

As she drove prayerfully along, she listened to a Phil Wickham CD and felt blessed. She was awash with both hope and joy.

"Dear God," she said, "when I see Mr. Barron—when I meet him, what should I say?"

"*TELL HIM THAT IT IS NOW TIME FOR HIM TO TURN HIS ENDEAVORS TOWARDS ME, HIS LORD.*"

Carla had butterflies in her stomach when she walked into the Fayetteville Public Library at 1:21 p.m.

The building was impressive, to say the least, and was a precious reminder of the power of God. She approached the Welcome Desk, where a man who looked to be about thirty, with a bushy black beard and soft eyes, was seated.

She asked him where the book reading was.

"Upstairs, in the Wal-Mart Community Room" he said, pointing to a stairway.

Feeling confident that this was a fitting way to please the Lord, Carla climbed the stairs and went where she was meant to go.

The room was large, with numerous chairs set up before a podium

There was a man standing at the opposite end of the room, near the podium. Two of the chairs near the front were occupied—one by a young woman with blue hair, glasses, and a dreamcatcher necklace, another by a large man with a moustache who was wearing a Motörhead T-shirt. The man standing at the opposite end of the room was wearing a red plaid shirt and had an eye-patch over one eye.

Carla immediately recognized him from the profile photo on his Twitter account, though in real life he was more attractive.

She was about to approach him, but then decided it would be better if she talked to him *after* the reading, and so she sat down towards the back of the room, somewhat apart from her fellow sojourners. Fifteen minutes went by, but, due to the workings of the Lord, no one else came, and Laird Barron commenced his reading. Within minutes of hearing his voice, Carla knew that he was the instrument the Lord had intended for her. He read for about forty-five minutes, in a soothing, steady tone. As he read, Carla pressed her hands tightly in front of herself. She had goosebumps. She had never felt more loved in her entire life.

When Laird Barron had finished reading, everyone in the audience, including Carla, clapped. Then the two fellow sojourners who were sitting towards the front of the room got up and approached the author. The young woman with blue hair had him sign a book which she had in her possession, after which the large man wearing the Motörhead T-shirt stood exchanging words with him.

Carla arose from her seat and walked forward. Both men looked at her.

"Hey, I gotta take a piss," she overheard the large man tell the author. "Meet you downstairs?"

"Yeah," Barron said. "Give me five minutes."

It was then that Carla approached Laird Barron.

"Mr. Barron," she said.

"Yeah," he replied, "thanks for coming to the reading. I hope I didn't disappoint."

A faint smell of whisky lurked about his person.

Carla handed him the manuscript of *The Doorman*.

"What's this?" he asked.

"It's my work in progress, *The Doorman*. I would feel blessed if you'd read it."

"Is it horror?"

Carla smiled.

"Mr. Barron," she said, "now is the time for you to begin your battle with the enemy and your service towards our Lord, Jesus Christ. Without God, you will never truly find joy."

"I don't usually read people's manuscripts. You might consider showing it to an, um, agent."

"Please, Mr. Barron, don't be indifferent to the King. He wants *you* to glorify *Him*. I didn't come before you solely due to the whim of my heart. I didn't come just to listen to a fellow author, but because Jesus is the author of my faith. God called me to do it. My contact details are on the top, right-hand corner of the first page. It is true that *The Doorman* is a work in progress, but the Lord knows that so are our lives."

As she drove back to Rose Bud, with the sweet afternoon light pouring over the highway, she felt confident that her work would, in the end, bear godly fruit and, indeed, it was so.

In the coming season of her life Laird Barron, having read *The Doorman* and gained faith therein, promoted her work greatly, securing her with a contract with a small but reputable publishing house, and, after the miraculous event had happened, helping her broadcast the good word through both social media and conventions. The film rights to her book were purchased by a well-known director and the there was a strong likelihood that *The Doorman* would, in time, become a major motion picture.

"I guess it's true then," Wyatt said.

"What's true, Wyatt?" Carla asked.

"That God only makes happy endings."

Love Charm

1.

"Spells? You mean like, um, dizzy spells?"

"No," Liam said to the librarian, "I mean magic spells."

The librarian was a man who looked to be about thirty with a bushy black beard and soft eyes. He turned towards the other librarian who was seated near him, an older man with white hair and glasses.

"Do we have any books on magic spells, Ron?"

"He needs to check the catalog." Ron looked up at Liam. "Go check the catalog. Just type in 'spells' and see what comes up."

It had been some time since Liam had been to the library. He had never been much of a reader really, preferring to watch DVDs or play video games in his spare time.

He wondered if he should have told the librarians the exact kind of spell he was looking for. Maybe if they had known it was for a love spell, they would have been more helpful.

He walked over to the computer catalog, typed the word 'spells' in, and a number of titles came up.

"*Word Nerd: Dispatches from the Games, Grammar, and Geek Underground,*" he read.

No, that didn't sound right.

"*The Book of She: Your Heroine's Journey into the Heart of Feminine Power.*"

And neither did that.

"*My Dog May be a Genius: Poem. . . . Dorrie and the Haunted Schoolhouse . . . Ms. Wiz Spells Trouble . . . D.A.N.G.E.R. Spells the Hangman . . .*"

He read through about thirty similar titles and finally came across one which seemed promising:

"*The Amanaska Tantra.*"

He liked the sound of the word 'tantra'. He wasn't sure what it meant, but he remembered that it had something to do with love. He jotted down the call number on a little sheet of paper that was near the computer and then went and got the book from the stacks.

It was much older than he had expected it to be and didn't have a picture on the cover.

He looked at the printing date and saw that it had been printed in 1946 in Gauhati, India, by the Assam Government Press. It didn't list an author, but said it had been translated to English by Pandit Angaraag Goswami Nechim. Looking at the index he saw that there were, in fact, lots of spells and strange recipes.

"It must be the real thing," he thought and decided to check it out.

When Liam got home, twenty minutes later, he poured himself a glass of Zinfandel, grabbed a bag of organic corn chips, went to the couch and opened the book.

He began to read the forward:

> The text of this book is taken from a copy made in 1906, by Dr. Gummadi Lagadapati, from the original, which was written in ancient Assamese on oblong strips of sanchi bark and was in the possession of a branch of the Rajaputin family of Tumudibandh. This family was able to trace their history back to the Pradyota dynasty. The text is thought to be not less than 700 years old. It is probably a translation into Assamese of an older Sanskrit work of the same title. Efforts have been made to obtain the original but without success. Evidently the book is kept in great secrecy and from the contents it appears that there is much justification for keeping it so.

"Wow," Liam said out loud and, while nibbling on a corn chip, turned to the back of the book, to the index.

There were, as he had already noticed, lots of spells and recipes listed—spells for finding hidden treasure, for taking revenge on one's neighbor, for winning at dice, for making oneself invisible, for dumbfounding one's opponent, for causing people to argue.

Finally he came to exactly what he had been hoping for, a 'Spell to Subdue a Girl and Make Her Love You':

> First a mystical diagram of a twelve-pointed star with a heptagon in the center should be drawn with the blood of the third finger of the right hand on a piece of bhurjjapatra (birch wood). The name of the girl who is desired to be subdued should be written inside the diagram with the blood of the big toe of the right foot and then chanted one thousand times. Once this is done, the charm should be suspended by a piece of string made from the tail hairs of a two-year-old stallion and worn around the neck. The woman whose name is written therein will become subdued like a slave at the sight of it.

Liam suddenly realized that casting a spell was a lot more complicated than he had thought.

"Well, if it was easy to win Amy's love, it wouldn't be worth it," he said to himself in a determined voice.

He had been struck by Amy the first time he saw her. She wasn't what one would traditionally call beautiful, but she had a certain quality about her that attracted Liam in ways he had never been attracted before. He often dreamed about them cuddling or cooking together. He would give her foot massages and they would discuss psychology.

He had never, previously, really considered himself the romantic type, but once he met Amy he had come to realize that he was the most romantic man in the world. He was a bit worried about coming right out and saying how he felt, so he had begun to stalk her on social media. Under an assumed name he friended her on Facebook and followed her Twitter account—though, truth be told, she seldom tweeted.

At work he had several times been about to ask her if she would join him for a cup of coffee, but her gaze, haughty and sharp, had always frightened him away. If, over the weekend, he could make the charm, however, on Monday things would be different. She would be asking *him*, if *he* wanted coffee—and probably a lot more.

Yes, using magic to win her love was a lot more complicated than he had anticipated, and making the charm would be no easy matter. Four points, however, were in his favor:

1. In his back yard a birch tree, by chance, was growing.
2. Back in high school he had taken a wood shop class, where, over the course of a semester, he and a classmate, whose name was Rahmonberdi Smith, had constructed a dog house.
3. In his garage he had a whole series of saws and chisels which he had bought, thinking that one day he would take up carpentry as a hobby.
4. He lived only three miles from the Golden Circle Riding Stables.

2.

"What do you mean? Does he, like, say weird things to you?"

"No, nothing like that. But his eyes are always following me and a few people at work have told me that he's crazy about me."

"What kind of a person is he?"

"I don't really know. He's not bad looking, but he seems pretty square."

"Nothing wrong with being square," Raychel said.

She was wearing a tank top and no bra and had tattoos running from her wrists all the way up her arms.

"Yeah," Amy replied, "there's nothing wrong with being square, but this guy makes me uncomfortable. It isn't like he's fallen in love with me because he knows me, because he knows what kind of a person I am or what is in my mind. It's just one of those creepy infatuations."

There was still a third of the bottle of wine left and Raychel divvied it up between their two glasses.

"If you want to solve the problem, I think I can help," she said, taking a sip from her glass.

"What do you mean?"

"You did know that I was heavy into Wicca, right?"

"Well, yeah, sort of I guess, but, um—well, that stuff's not real, is it?"

"Jeez, everyone is so materialistic! People gulp down Prozac and Zostavax no problem and then act like herblore and crystals, which have, like, been around since time began, are bullshit. I mean, if you don't click with what I'm saying, that's fine, but I think you're missing out on a real opportunity."

Amy took a drink of wine and held the glass poised in front of her chin, which was rather large. She had a thoughtful look on her face. Whatever else she was, she was not a closed-minded person. She had once cured herself of a cold by putting onion in her socks, so maybe wicca wasn't so far-fetched after all.

"Do you really think you can help me?" she asked.

"Look, babe, I'll make a spell for you so this creep leaves you alone."

"Leaves me alone?"

"Yes, we can cast a hate spell—like, summon the demon of hate and put her in a hate charm. It will make that jerk hate you."

"Well, I don't really need him to hate me."

"It's better than him having a crazy crush on you, isn't it?"

"Much."

"So, there's your answer."

Amy thought about it for another minute or so, and then agreed.

They polished off the wine in their glasses, got up from their chairs and Raychel led her into a small room in the back of the house that she had never been in before.

"Welcome to my broom closet," Raychel said.

Raychel took out a BIC lighter and lit a number of colored wisdom candles that were placed about the room, thus shedding dancing light on:

High vibration crystals
And crop-circle stones;
Amethyst pendulums;
Jars of elderberries
And jezebel root;
A wood triquetra ritual box
And a bottle
Of vetivert oil.

"Just wait a minute while I change into my witch rags," Raychel said and left Amy standing alone.

The room was full of what was just mentioned and all sorts of other things, and Amy, enchanted, looked about, investigating here and there.

Some of Raychel's oil paintings were on the walls. One of them showed a magical blue female petting a wolf, another was a depiction of Cleopatra basking apocalyptically with a jellyfish in neon light.

Amy had always been somewhat jealous of her friend's artistic talent.

Turning to some shelves, she saw a stack of Lenormand cards, a few wands, a book on Mayan shamanism, some crow feathers, a smoky obsidian angel, and a string of Earth spirit pagan prayer beads.

At one end of the room was an altar on which were placed a silver-plated chalice with a spiraling stem, a piece of driftwood, a triple-moon altar bell, a pair of Renaissance bodice dagger scissors in a sheath decorated with red jewels, a cat carved out of a piece of rowan wood, and an abalone shell incense burner partially filled with light blue incense burner sand. In front of the altar was a small table, with a pentagram cushion to sit on placed in front of that.

When Raychel came back in, she was wearing a robe made of 100% bamboo fiber. Around her waist was a non-metallic gold sash. She had combed out her hair so it fell in long, black ribbons over her shoulders and chest and a yellow rose was planted in the hair above her forehead. Amy was quite impressed.

"Okay, let's do this thing!" Raychel said as she lit a stick of Egyptian Goddess incense and planted it in the light blue incense burner sand in the abalone shell incense burner on the altar.

She went over to a shelf and took down a winged fairy Raku clay bottle.

"What's that?"

"It's special water. I gathered it from seven different churches and mixed it together with some menstrual blood."

"You really take this stuff seriously, don't you?"

"A real witch has to, honey."

Raychel took up a small black stone and showed it to Amy.

"This is a stone I picked up while doing a meditation walk last summer when I was on vacation in Oregon. I felt a strong power emanating from it and knew that it wanted to help me. It's going to be the hex."

"Cool."

"This male, Liam, what's his last name?"

"Stoltenberg."

Raychel nodded her head and gathered up a piece of parchment, a peacock feather quill and a bottle of ink and put them on the table in front of Amy.

"This is bat's blood ink. Just dip the quill in there and write what I tell you."

Amy agreed, and Raychel, in a vibrant yet somber voice, began to dictate:

"I, Sister Amy, do make this charm, summoning Sister Goddess, our Sister Demon Erida, who men for time immemorial have never understood, to cause hate in the breast of Liam Stoltenberg. Swarm your sweet butterflies, Erida, my dear, and make this male hate me, Amy Adachi. Yes, he must hate me, like worms hate the sun, like cockroaches hate the smell of sweet flowers, like dirty little boys hate hot soapy baths. Erida! Erida! Erida, daughter of the Night and mother of Quarrels and Battles, mother of Anarchy and Manslaughter—Erida, you beautiful lady of relentless wrath, let it be so!"

Raychel took the paper and burnt it in a green marble onyx ritual bowl. Then she mixed in with the ashes some of the liquid from the winged fairy Raku clay bottle and rubbed the mixture over the stone.

Raychel waved her hands over the stone. A low whining sound was coming from her throat.

"Okay, the demon is in the stone now," she said a moment later.

"You mean . . . ?"

"Yeah, Erida. She'll make Liam hate you. She's in the stone now."

"You sure?"

"Absolutely. Basically you need to get this on Liam's person or as close to it as possible."

"I don't really want to touch his person."

"What's his workspace like?"

"Just a desk with a computer on it and a bottle of Dasani water."

"Okay, put it behind the computer monitor."

"And he'll start to hate me?"

"Yup."

3.

On Monday morning, Liam woke up at slightly after seven and had a cup of coffee, a bowl of granola with a banana cut up in it, 500 mg of vitamin C; had shaved, showered and brushed his teeth by ten to eight. He climbed into a pair of jeans, put on a button-up shirt and a pair of Scandinavian leather shoes, and then picked up the love charm he had made over the weekend.

It was probably a lot bigger than it should have been—a block of wood about 4 × 6 inches and about an inch thick—but it was the first love charm he had ever made and he was not without his pride.

"I sure hope this works," he thought as he put it around his neck. He tucked it into his button-up shirt, deciding that it would be best not to reveal it until Amy was in his presence.

He got in his Kona-blue Ford Focus, put the key in the ignition, twisted it, and reversed out of his driveway.

A quarter of an hour later, he was downtown, turning the corner onto the street where he worked.

Though he loved his job, he hated the fact that they had no employee parking. Yes, there were a few spots for the top people, but the rest were forced to either park in a parking garage four blocks away that charged eighteen dollars a day, or park on the street where they had to pay a quarter for every fifteen minutes. Luckily the meters had a four-hour maximum, so he was able to put four dollars in in the morning, then return during his lunch break and feed the meter again. It was true that some employees took public transportation, but he liked the freedom of driving himself.

He was lucky. He found a space right in front of the building and slid into it.

He always kept a few rolls of quarters in his front door storage bin for parking. He took a handful of quarters, got out of the car and went to the meter. He stuck a quarter in, but it didn't register.

"Fucking meter," he said.

He knocked the meter with the heel of the palm of his hand, but it still didn't register.

He wondered if he should look for another parking spot or try his luck with another quarter. He looked around, but didn't see any free spots. He looked at his watch. It was 8:27, just three minutes before he was supposed to be in the office. If he went looking for another spot, he would probably be a few minutes late, and he hated being late. He had, in fact, only been late twice since he had started working at Magnum Services three years before.

He put another quarter in the meter but it still didn't register. Now he was really ticked off. The meter had already eaten fifty cents and he was going to be late if it didn't get its ass in gear.

He hit the meter lightly with the palm of his hand, and then hit it again, much harder.

Just then there was a brief whooping sound. Liam looked over and saw a police cruiser pull up. Its lights were flashing and a police officer jumped out of the car. The officer had greenish eyes and very thin lips.

"The meter ate two of my quarters," Liam told the officer.

"You were trying to break it and take the coins, weren't you?"

"No, I work here and was just parking."

"You were trying to damage City property."

"I guess when someone wears a tin badge they think they're God," Liam said quietly.

"What?"

"Nothing."

"I heard what you said."

"Whatever."

"Sir, I'm placing you under arrest."

"Huh?"

"Please step away from the meter."

"I have to get to work!" Liam pleaded.

"You should have thought about that before you decided to damage public property."

4.

The police-person pulled into the back of the station, opened the back door of the police car, and led Liam in.

A few uniformed police-people were standing around, drinking cups of Starbucks coffee and eating scones.

"What you got there?"

"This individual was destroying City property and then became verbally abusive towards me."

One of the police officers smiled at Liam, but the others frowned. Liam wondered what the officer who smiled would look like out of uniform, but then banished the thought.

"I have to find Amy," he murmured to himself.

When they booked Liam, they made him empty his pockets and asked him to remove any watch or jewelry he might be wearing. Reluctantly, Liam removed the love charm from his neck and set it down on the desk with his other personal effects. The booking officer looked at the square of wood hanging by a hand-rolled string of horse tail hair.

"What's this?"

"Just a thing."

"Are you an artist?"

"It's just something I made."

"A woman's name is written on it."

"Yeah, um, a friend . . ."

The cell Liam was put in was quite small. The only thing in it was a toilet without a toilet seat and two other men, who were seated on the floor.

"Hey," Liam said.

"Welcome to paradise."

The one who had greeted him, in a gruff voice that sounded like it had been exhumed from desert earth, was a rangy fellow who looked to be about thirty-two, with a large nose jutting out over a scraggly red moustache. The other man, who just nodded at Liam, was nondescript.

Liam sat down on the floor.

The man with the red moustache, whose name was Donatas, asked him what he was there for, and Liam told him.

"Destruction of City property and disorderly conduct," Donatas repeated.

"And you?" Liam asked.

"Trespassing."

"They can arrest you for that?"

"I guess so. I was just walking around in an open field . . ."

"And him?" Liam asked, nodding towards the nondescript man.

"Ask him."

"And you?" Liam said.

"Magic."

"Magic?"

"Yeah, I had a spell put on me."

"Not good," Donatas said.

"What kind of spell?" Liam asked.

"Quite a story. . . . It all began—well . . . I work as a host over at Carrabba's Bar and Grill . . . so my hours are somewhat irregular and it's long been a challenge for me to balance work life and personal life. Fortunately, however, Carrabba's celebrates an inclusive culture, which welcomes and embraces our collective differences. Anyhow, after spending my evenings opening the door for departing and arriving guests, seating them in a friendly manner, assisting in maintaining the overall guest-flow of the restaurant, ensuring that all reservations, telephone calls, and take-out procedures are followed, and properly handling cash and credit cards for all transactions within the restaurant, I would come home, feed my dog, whose name is Eagle, and take a little time watching the late shows on TV."

"Sounds like a pretty good life," Donatas said.

"Yeah, it *was* a good life, until *she* moved in across the street."

"*She?*"

"Yes. She was my age or a little younger. A real hotty. She pulled up one day in a Penske truck and, with a couple of chick friends in jeans, started unloading her stuff. She was wearing a dragonfly dreamcatcher T-shirt and didn't appear to be wearing a bra, so I went over and offered to help, and moved some stuff in. After a while, they offered to smoke some marijuana with me, but I declined."

"Not into the weed?" Donatas asked.

"Naw, makes me paranoid."

"I get that," Liam said.

"Anyhow, after she moved in, things started to change. . . . I would come home and Eagle would be there whining for me. I'd give her some milk and she'd calm down but then start whining again. About two weeks in, I was out front watering my yard and my neighbor was fucking around with some tomato plants in hers. We got to talking and she invited me over for a glass of wine and I thought why not. The truth is, that I've been looking for a mating partner for some time, but with my work schedule it's been difficult."

"Would think you'd meet a lot of chicks over at Carrabba's," Donatas said.

"Life's funny that way, isn't it? I went on vacation once to Costa Rica, where, you know, they grow some of the best coffee in the world. But the people living there only drank instant coffee. They couldn't drink the coffee that grew right there in front of them. Working at Carrabba's is like that."

"Fucking capitalism."

"Yeah, well . . . my neighbor and I were drinking this wine, and wine is, as we all know, a catalyst to other things. She was wearing a green lightweight crinkle cotton skirt with purple pentagrams on it and a tank top and . . ."

"No bra?"

". . . and no bra. And, well, we were just chit-chatting, talking about different things, like how it's okay to give and receive affection, how sometimes a person has to showcase their naked self, and things like that, and, well, then she started talking about Silver RavenWolf and asking if I had read her and I told her that in my relax time I mainly liked to watch TV. and wasn't too interested in books. After that things noticeably cooled and I went home the same man I had come and in the days that followed strange things started to happen."

"Yeah?"

"Yeah. I found a dead cat in my mailbox, then, a few days later, a bunch of peculiar rocks on my lawn and after that some women's panties appeared on my doorstep with a note pinned to them that said 'living things make choices'."

"She probably wanted you, dude. She invited you over for wine and you failed to make the situation escalate."

"Yeah, well, maybe. Anyhow, the morning after the women's panties appeared I woke up and started to hear weird knocking sounds coming from the walls and one of the cushions from my couch in the living room had moved into the bathroom. I looked outside and there was my neighbor, standing there staring at my house. That's when I knew, with total certainty, that she was putting a spell on me."

"So what did you do?"

"I called the cops."

"Not exactly a boss move," Donatas said.

"Yeah, well, making mistakes is part of being human. . . . I stood at the window and waited for the cops to come, and they did. But instead of going to her house, they came to mine and knocked on the door. They came inside and started looking around and found a bunch of crystal meth in my freezer. But it wasn't mine. Someone else had put it there!"

There was a moment of silence.

"It's that craving," Donatas said, presently.

"Craving?"

"For intimacy. We try to do things, to take care of our needs without abandoning the core social skills that let us function. . . . . Emotional intelligence. . . . Join a video game community or start going to the gym. Romantic achievements aren't for everyone. For a chick to make you happy, you gotta have happiness in yourself. It takes a lot of courage. . . . It takes courage to even hug someone—for a guy to admit to himself that is all he really wants is to cuddle and——"

Just then the door to the cell opened. A corrections officer was standing there.

"Liam Stoltenberg?" the corrections officer said.

"Yeah?" Liam replied, standing up.

"You'll have to come with me."

The corrections officer led Liam down a long, well-lit hallway—and from somewhere, Liam was unsure where, *there was the sound of dull moaning.*

The Giant Horse

In the deserts of Mexico, there was a little cabin. It had one window and a chimney and a very poor internet connection. Inside the cabin lived Demián Lopez Lanús, the Rainbow-Colored Mummy.

He would walk through the desert, looking for food. He ate cactus fruit and pine nuts. Sometimes he found lizards and ate them too. He had mummy magic, and when he blew, the desert was covered with dust storms.

But Demián was very lonely, because he had no friends. When he walked up to someone, they got scared and ran away. Even the donkeys and rabbits and USBP did not want to talk to him.

Demián was sad and wanted to cry. But mummies don't cry, especially those that are rainbow-colored.

One day when Demián was walking through the desert, a big crow came and landed in front of him.

"Hello," the crow said, "my name is Allan Blum."

"My name is Demián."

"I come from Canada," Allan, the crow said. "I'm a bandit."

"I come from here," Demián replied. "I come from Mexico. I'm a rainbow-colored mummy."

"Why are you so sad?" Allan asked.

"Because I'm lonely out here in the desert. People run away from me and don't want to talk."

"Have you tried meeting people through the internet?"

"I have a Tinder account, but no one seems interested."

"So sad."

"Yeah."

"You're a mummy, so you should do what you want to. I'll be your friend. Listen to me and we can make a lot of money."

Demián was happy and told the crow he would do what he wanted.

Allan flew up into the air and, after about an hour, came back.

"A group of men is coming," he said. "They are riding mules and look like they have money. Let's scare them and take what they have."

At this point Brendan Connell put down his pen. He was rather tired of writing these "pleasant" stories. In fact, he wouldn't be doing it at all if Justin Isis, realizing what a "pleasant" fellow he was, hadn't been insisting for some time that he write a "collection" of Pleasant Tales. And then there was the publisher, the chief editor of which had been sending him eager messages through Facebook for months asking when "the book" would be completed.

Brendan yawned, took out his iPhone and looked at it. It too seemed rather uninteresting, a storehouse of non-existent synthetic objects. He opened his e-mail, but amidst the numerous alerts from left wing political "organizations", European airlines and online "poetry" magazines, he found nothing to draw him out of his "ennui", and had the same sort of performative role as the horns of a cat or the disobedient children of a barren woman.

"I should probably get the fuck out of the house," he said to himself.

He put on his shoes, a pair of Rockports he had bought for cheap at a discount clothing outlet a few months before, and headed out the door.

The neighborhood had changed a lot in recent years, and Brendan walked through it with a mixture of regret and nostalgia, reflecting on the ontological inseperability of his metaphysical being and the existential qualifications of his surroundings. Coming to the train tracks, he turned towards downtown. He passed the local brewery, but did not enter, as their beer tended to give him a headache and act as a complete negation of the spiritual universe.

He proceeded on, along the railroad tracks, until he came to Montezuma Avenue and then took a right. Passing by a movie theater, he noticed that the wall had been blessed with some graffiti—some freshly painted mermaid porn that had been unskillfully scrawled over the stucco. It would have been hard to call his perceptual experiences *pleasant*, but at least he was getting some fresh air. He took out his iPhone, snapped a photo, and was just about to send it to his friend Quentin, when he saw that he had a fresh e-mail. It was from the public library and informed him that an interlibrary loan book he had ordered, *The School Sayings of Confucius*, had arrived and was ready for pick-up.

Nothing suited his schedule better.

He ventured further along Montezuma Ave. until he came to Guadalupe Street, at which he took a left, heading north, the snow-coated breasts of the mountains visible in the distance. After about a third of a mile, he came to West San Francisco Street and turned right. He proceeded on for two-tenths of a mile, and was just passing by Starbucks, when he heard a tapping on the window and, looking over, noticed a bearded man motioning him to enter. He did and, a moment later, was shaking hands with Jim Whitefather.

"Hey, brother, I thought it was you passing by, but wasn't sure. You look older."

"Yeah."

Jim looked older too. A streak of white ran through his beard, and he didn't have much hair left on his head. Jim had gained fame due to the collection of short fiction he had published a few years earlier, *Horrible Things Happen*, which had won wide acclaim throughout the horror circuit for combining contemporary family drama with monstrous supernatural motifs.

"I'm just here doing some writing," Jim said, motioning towards his open laptop. "Drinking some joe, thanks to my AMAZING daughter. It was my birthday a few days ago. Turned forty-eight. She gave me a twenty-five dollar Starbucks gift card. Want something?"

"Um, sure. Sort of feel like something soft, mellow and flavorful."

"A cup of Blonde Roast?"

"Okay."

"Scone?"

"Nah."

Jim went up to the counter and got a dumpy-looking girl who seemed unreasonably cheerful to make Brendan a cup of coffee. The latter, having received this pleasant handcrafted beverage, asked Jim what was "new".

Jim nodded towards his laptop, on which a Word document was open.

"I've really been struggling with this text. It makes me feel like, you know, maybe I'm not really a writer. Before this, I was writing a werewolf story with two gay men as the protagonists. I had got as far as the first sex scene, which I wanted to make a bit graphic, sort of like *Brokeback Mountain*, but with more passion, but I couldn't get the mechanics right, so I trashed it."

"Shouldn't do that."

"The mechanics . . . were very complicated."

"What are you writing about now?"

"It's sort of a Kafkaesque pulp piece. . . . Have had to do a lot of research. Do you mind if I read you what I have so far? I know you're a big fan of The Russians—you know, Dostoevsky, Nabokov—that sort of thing—so you might like it. But I'm feeling grave uncertainties about my writing."

Brendan said he would be happy to offer his opinion, and so Jim read to him the following:

"Who was here first?" the man behind the counter asked, turning around.

"I was," Riaan replied and set two six-packs of Molson's Extra Gold down beside the cash register along with a copy of the *South Milwaukee Post Journal Sentinel*.

The other man, the one with the ponytail and yellow-tinted glasses, did not say anything, though in reality he had already been waiting at the counter when Riaan walked up. He merely set his thin lips together and bent his head down, his hand tense around a quart carton of milk.

Riaan left the market, crossed the street and climbed into the cab of his red Dodge Caravan. He had bought the car the year before, shortly after meeting Linda—after she had told him in a fit of hot zeal that *she wanted to have his baby.*

But she had only said this once, and the vehicle, though certainly versatile, had a lot more interior space than he actually needed.

"Quarter to three," he said, looking at his watch. "I still have fifteen minutes."

He opened a Molson's Extra Gold, took a sip and then began to read the paper. He felt a certain thrill in merely existing—a thrill that had gradually become less thrilling over the last few months—ever since he had realized that Linda had lost her attraction for him. Would it be a repeat of what had occurred with his ex-wife, when she had let him go for a woman—a woman much younger than he—one in better shape, with a tattoo of a dreamcatcher on her thigh? After drinking two beers and reading the home and garden section, Riaan climbed back out of the truck, re-crossed the street and entered the tattoo shop which was next door to the market.

"How goes it?" Riaan asked, taking off his hat and jacket and hanging them on the coat rack.

"Greetings," the man, whose name was Bill, replied.

Bill was a big fellow with a handlebar moustache, a tank-top shirt and richly tattooed arms. A young man lay bare-backed on the table in front of him, a yellow and blue, half-finished design of the logo of the Marquette Golden Eagles on his shoulder.

"Wasn't my appointment for three?" Riaan asked.

"Sure," Bill replied, biting at his moustache. "My assistant Igor—Igor Collins—will take care of you. I showed him the design you want, so he's all ready. Don't worry, Igor's a master. The bitches will be crawling all over you."

The man with the ponytail and yellow-tinted glasses appeared from the back room, an open carton of milk in his hand. He took a sip, licked his lips and said, in a quiet, somewhat foreign sounding voice, "Mr. Riaan? Come this way, please."

Riaan followed him into the back room, which was dark except for a single, bright photographer's lamp poised over a cushioned, linen covered table.

"I'm sorry about what happened earlier," Riaan said nervously, unbuttoning his shirt. "I guess I was in a sour mood. I've been having trouble with my girlfriend, so . . ."

"So?"

"So, no hard feelings, right?"

"Hard feelings? Of course not. Be calm, my *friend*," the other man said quietly, his thin lips ironically curling. "Now, if you would be so kind as to lay on the table, I will begin."

Riaan climbed onto the table, his corduroy pants tight around his rather full hips, and lay down on his stomach. When he had first met Linda through OkCupid, and had asked her what kind of men she liked, she had told him that she liked 'country types' and 'bad boys' and she was a big fan of Bucky Covington. Riaan suspected that this was part of the reason she had not wanted to make love for the past two months. It was time for him to change his image. If she wanted a bad boy, *he would be that bad boy.*

"So you think you can do the cowboy okay?" he asked, stretching out his left arm.

"Yes. Cowboy with guns, lasso and purple flower."

"And the cigar, and lots of smoke. And the name 'Linda' on the petals of the flower. And a horse's skull. And a bright green snake."

"Yes, Mr. Riaan, I have the design right here. Guns, lasso and bright green snake. On your upper arm, correct?"

"On my left bicep—right here."

"Left bicep. Correct, sir. I will begin," Igor said in his quiet, oily voice.

He worked with surprising agility, his needle gracefully inking out the lines on Riaan's skin. Every now and again he would pause, take a sip of his milk and lick the residue from his lips with a darting, extraordinarily red tongue. Riaan could not see the man's eyes behind the thick yellow lenses of his glasses, and was surprised that Igor could see well enough to do the delicate operation.

Jim had finished reading. A few drops of sweat had formed over his hairless forehead. He looked at Brendan with eager eyes.

"What do you think?" he asked.

"It's great!" Brendan replied.

Jim smiled, gave a short laugh, nodded his head and then shook it.

"You really like it?" he asked.

Brendan said that, yes, he did really like it.

"I guess, at the end, he is found dead somewhere hanging by a rope?" he added.

A worried expression invaded Jim's round face. "Is that too . . . obvious?" he asked.

"Not at all. I just happen to be practicing Ching Ts'en's method of precognition."

A few minutes later, Brendan was exiting Starbucks and, a moment after that, he was passing through the Plaza, inhaling the corresponding truth of the fajita cart and translating it into his fictional universe and recognizing the problematic dualism of his wants and his needs.

Due to the residue of antecedent events, his footsteps led him naturally to the public library, which was just about four stone throws from the Plaza. He entered.

A man who looked to be about thirty with a bushy black beard and soft eyes was stationed at the reference desk. Noiselessly Brendan handed him his library card and even more noiselessly the man handed Brendan a large orange volume that contained inside it the sayings of Master Kong.

Brendan then stepped back, feeling a sudden emptiness within himself. He could return home. Or get a Frito pie. Or, as he sometimes did, study the library's recent acquisitions.

He wandered over to the section where the new arrivals were stacked, their spines lined up like countless moats—some filled with snakes, others hot oil; some with tarantulas, others worm-filled excrement.

"I wish I didn't have so many unpleasant thoughts," Brendan murmured to himself, as he reached for a volume.

It was by an American feminist writer who had attended the Iowa Writers' Workshop.

Brendan opened the book to a random page somewhere in the middle and read:

> On the street, I try so hard, to be aware of only me,
> the shop windows, not the eyes, that look, and pierce—
> those of poor males, rags, the seer and the seen. . . . But
> she, where is she that claims to love, has let me explore,
> that my breath breathes because of? Yes, she is that
> animal for which I wander, sacrifice all pride, happily,
> such torture. Though these streets are nothing—one
> day they will be the shards of a lost civilization—I will
> remain erect, beautiful in my anguish, and will not be
> crushed, renounce all hope. This is a city for conquest,
> but I will not conquer, only want, want that gratification,
> harmless human pleasures . . . not for procreation and

. . . and my body is a lovely flower. . . . An orchid that raises its petals, its fragile stamens, to the touch of her mortality, the dear.

Brendan nodded his head and replaced the book on the shelf, then picked up another and another and another—all of them by people with BAs and MFAs—Clarion Writers' Workshop alumni and people who had attended Johns Hopkins Writing Seminars or NEOMFA—a seemingly endless train of rather flat, rather competent prose that marched forward with the well-regulated steps of an army—an army of fiction based neither on inspiration, nor talent, nor experience—but simply on the need to fulfill their cycles—like salmon madly swimming upstream to spawn. . . .

"It's funny," he thought. "I'm writing this story and yet I'm doing the exact same things I do in real life. I'm being *way* too critical, and there's really no need. I should be having more fun."

Just then he noticed that he was surrounded by beautiful women— lots of them. Some had three breasts, some were dressed in shear pink sheathes—others naked, their bodies dripping with oil of civet, their sexual organs emitting rays of soothing light—and others, again, whose waists were so slim that they were almost invisible and whose breasts were so large that they shone resplendent like moons or planets plucked from some forgotten science fiction film. All of them—all of those joyous women who swayed like wheat in the wind—were eyeing him hungrily and in their eyes were reflected ponds of variegated jewels surrounded by exotic flowers of countless variety and their mouths smiled—their teeth like swans, their tongues gorgeous red blossoms.

Then, while wonderful music was being played by tiny musicians sitting on only slightly less tiny clouds, the crowd of women parted and one woman, more beautiful than the rest, moved forward with short, undulating strides, like those of a goose—and she carried a platinum tray encrusted with pearls—and on the tray was a book with the best cover ever—and she approached—and she approached—and with her lovely chin pointed towards the book—and Brendan, reaching forward, picked it up. . . . He turned to the introduction and read the first lines, which promised of greater things within:

What is the opposite of Horror?

It cannot be, as is often thought, an unreflective grounding in the everyday, the kind of consensus-seeking Social Realism favored by whoever currently maintains the Canon™. Inasmuch as Horror is a scalar value, a jerking left into the negative zone of the Uncanny, then its opposite cannot be the zero point neutrality of the merely Real; it requires, instead, a state just as heightened, equal but opposite. . . .